# THE CENTRAL SCHOOL OF SPEECH AND DRAMA

## UNIVERSITY OF LONDON

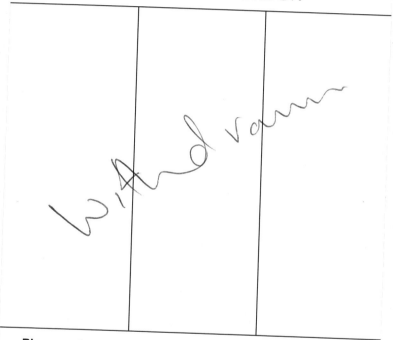

**Please return or renew this item by the last date shown.**

The Library, Central School of Speech and Drama,
Embassy Theatre, Eton Avenue, London, NW3 3HY
http://heritage.cssd.ac.uk
library@cssd.ac.uk
Direct line: 0207 559 3942

# A MAP OF NOWHERE

# A Map of
# Nowhere

Gillian Cross

Oxford University Press
*Oxford Toronto Melbourne*

Oxford University Press, Walton Street, Oxford OX2 6DP

*Oxford New York Toronto*
*Delhi Bombay Calcutta Madras Karachi*
*Petaling Jaya Singapore Hong Kong Tokyo*
*Nairobi Dar es Salaam Cape Town*
*Melbourne Auckland*

and associated companies in
*Berlin Ibadan*

Oxford is a trade mark of Oxford University Press

British Library Cataloguing in Publication Data

Cross, Gillian
A map of nowhere.
I. Title
823'.914[J]

ISBN 0-19-271583-6

Typeset by Pentacor Ltd, High Wycombe, Bucks
Printed and bound in Great Britain by
Biddles Ltd, Guildford and King's Lynn

# Chapter 1

One ordinary Wednesday afternoon, after fourth-year football practice, Nick Miller opened his bag to chuck in his muddy boots—and saw a wallet inside. Not his wallet. It was a cheap brown plastic one, lying on top of everything, just under the opening of the zip. As if someone had dropped it in quickly while the changing room was empty.

Nick glanced round, to see if anyone was watching, but the others were all clustered at the far end of the changing room, listening to Livingstone's sick jokes about seals. Quietly Nick slid the wallet out and opened it.

It was labelled clearly enough. A neat square of cardboard had been slipped behind the little plastic window and the writing on it was in tidy capitals.

> JOSEPH FISHER,
> THE STORES,
> HOLNEY SEAS END,
> LINCS.

Nick struggled for a face to match the name. A tall skinny kid in the Fifth Year wasn't he? The sort of person you could prop in a corner and not notice for months except when he was being teased. Well, it would be interesting to see what he kept in his wallet. Nick flicked open the pocket that should have held notes. There was nothing in it except a folded piece of paper. A letter? An address? A shopping list? He took it out and unfolded it. It was covered with small neat writing.

> *Left hand tunnel: strange smells—corpses? giant maggots?—test for methane gas—lay trap.*
> *Right hand tunnel: sharply downhill—surface slippery—check state of tunnel walls and explore chances of using rope.*

It sounded like some kind of adventure game. But where could Fisher possibly play? The school adventure game club had folded when Benson left, and Nick hadn't been able to find another one since.

For a second he stared down at the writing, wondering. Then—as the others roared with laughter at the far end of the changing room—he pulled open the zip of the change pocket and tipped the contents into his hand.

Two pounds and thirty-two pence. Hardly worth the bother. He was on the verge of throwing the whole lot away in disgust when he felt something still in there, jammed up in one corner of the pocket. Not another coin. Keys? He wriggled a finger in to knock it out and it fell into his palm, small and heavy.

It was a little metal alloy figure. A dwarf type, with a long beard and a short thick sword. Someone had painted it very carefully, with a fine brush picking out the detail. Red beard, streaked with grey, brown leather jerkin and trousers and a silver sword. There were even tiny runes lettered in along the sword blade. It was better done than Nick's own precious Star Warrior, which stood on the chest of drawers in his bedroom.

So Joseph Fisher *was* into adventure games. For a moment, remembering what it was like to play, Nick was so envious that it made him feel sick. The excitement of going into the unknown. The way the strange, imaginary world painted itself inside your head while the Game Master was talking. The cheerful, joking companionship of the adventurers. He missed it a lot, now he had no one to play with.

While he was still staring at the dwarf, he heard feet behind him, coming from the other end of the changing room. He shoved the dwarf into the wallet and the wallet back into his bag, as Livingstone yelled in his ear.

'I said—are you coming, Miller? Or do you fancy kipping down here until after half term?'

Nick pulled on his shoes and grinned. 'Oh, I dunno. Might not be such a bad idea. We could really work the place over with six days to ourselves. Strip everything out and sell it. We could be in the Bahamas by the time anyone noticed.'

'Oh sure,' jeered Parker, coming up behind Livingstone. 'Hear that, you guys? Miller reckons there's a market for antique computers.'

2

'Don't forget the video,' Nick said solemnly.

Everyone in the changing room collapsed into laughter. The video was a school joke. While Nick finished packing up his kit, the others went on adding to the plan, inventing more and more unlikely things to sell.

'—we could auction off the toilets—'

'—rent out the swimming pool as a rubbish tip—'

'—set up a fast-food restaurant in the home economics room—'

Livingstone snorted. 'What, with Sandra Parker as Head Chef?'

There were loud sick noises at the thought of food cooked by Parker's grubby sister. Parker himself made twice as much noise as anyone else, just to show he didn't have anything to do with her, and he went on after everyone else had finished, which was typical of him. He never knew when to stop.

Nick picked up his bag. 'Well, I'll leave you two to get on with the Great School Robbery, then. I'm going home. We're having a barbecue on Saturday, if the weather picks up.'

Livingstone grabbed Parker's ear and propelled him after Nick, towards the bicycle sheds, and the three of them unlocked their bikes and cycled down the High Street together.

'Going to ask us to your barbecue then?' Livingstone said, as they reached the end of Nick's road.

'Dunno.' Nick thought about it. 'Might do.'

'Your mum and dad always have the best barbecue food,' said Parker greedily. '*And* they don't mind if we have a few beers with it.'

He licked his fat lips and Nick wondered suddenly why he bothered hanging around with the two of them. They weren't interested in much except food and dirty jokes and they never had a good word to say for anyone else. Finding that wallet, with the dwarf in it, had reminded him what good times he and Benson used to have together, and it made him impatient.

'I'll phone you,' he muttered. 'OK?'

With a wave of his hand he turned the corner and cycled

3

off, forgetting all about both of them as soon as they were out of his sight. He was thinking about orcs and dragons. Vampires and werewolves and seven-headed hydras.

It was like being in another country. He cycled down the road automatically, barely noticing where he was going, and when he came round the bend to his own house he almost crashed into the motorbikes parked outside.

Terry's friends were there.

Nick looked carefully at the bikes. It wasn't all of them. Just the real close ones, the hard core. What he thought of, secretly, as The Company. It was easy to recognize Leo's Suzuki and Bill's battered old Kawasaki; and the big new Honda had to belong to Donna, Livingstone's sister. She'd been going on about getting a new one for six months.

Nick pushed his bicycle past them and down the driveway to the garage. No sign of either of the cars. Dad was away until tomorrow and Mum must be working a later shift. No wonder The Company had homed in on the house.

As he went in through the kitchen door, he could hear the music blaring from the lounge and the sound of Donna having one of her usual rows with Leo. Her voice rose sharply, spitting out swear words and Leo laughed as he answered, baiting her.

Then they all laughed.

When he had put the kettle on, Nick walked down the hall. The lounge door was open and he stopped in the doorway, not quite daring to go in. 'Anyone want a cup of coffee?'

Sometimes, if they said yes, he could stay when he brought the coffee back. Sit on the floor with his own cup, quietly, and imagine what it would be like to be one of them.

This looked like one of those good days. As he asked the question, Leo gave him a big, lazy smile and Terry shouted 'Great!' above the sound of the music. Going back to the kitchen, Nick grinned to himself.

But when he came through the hall again, they'd turned the music down and Donna had stopped pacing the room and settled on to Bill's chair with him. Somehow it was all more businesslike, as if they were getting ready to discuss something. Perhaps it would be better not to try and stay. Nick put the tray down on the coffee table, picked up his own cup and headed for the door.

'Hang on a minute,' Bill said, very quiet. He was always very quiet.

Nick stopped in the doorway and looked round. For a moment he felt as though they were all watching him. Then Terry said, 'Got your school bag anywhere around?'

'What for?'

'Bring it in,' said Bill. 'There's a good little boy.' He gave a quick nod, as if he wasn't expecting any hanging about, and Nick went into the kitchen.

'What's the matter?' he said as he came back swinging the bag. 'Fancy a bit of geography homework, do you? Missing school?'

'Do us a *favour*!' Donna pulled a face. Draining her beer, she lobbed the empty can into the pretty green satin waste-paper basket before she picked up her cup of coffee. 'We just want—a pencil and a ruler. Don't we?'

'That's right,' Terry said, watching Nick carefully.

'Going to lend us one?' Bill murmured.

It was all weird. There was something going on, something they all knew about and Nick didn't. For a moment he wondered what would happen if he refused to give them the pencil and ruler.

But that was daft. Nick couldn't see any harm in a pencil and a ruler, but he was dead sure there was a lot of harm in not doing what Bill asked him. And Terry and Donna could be pretty hard too, if they didn't get what they wanted. Putting his coffee down beside Leo's chair, he pulled open the zip of his bag.

Until that moment, Leo had been sprawled in his usual lazy pose, long legs stretched out, hands behind his head. But as Nick opened the zip he moved like lightning, leaning forward and whisking the bag out of his hands.

'What's this, then?' he said.

Dipping into the bag with long, strong fingers, he pulled out Joseph Fisher's wallet. Immediately, all the others gasped, as if they were shocked, and Terry grabbed Nick's shoulder.

5

'That's not yours, Nick. What are you doing with someone else's wallet?'

It was all a joke, it had to be a joke. They'd set him up by getting someone to plant the wallet in his bag, and now they were going to watch him squirm and try to get out of the awkward situation. That was the only sensible explanation. Nick grinned, a bit uneasily, and looked round at them all.

'What's up? You don't think I nicked it, do you?'

Leo smiled slowly. 'Well, we might. Depends what you were going to do with it, doesn't it?'

'Like what?' Nick said, puzzled.

'Like taking it back!' Sharply, Donna drained her cup of coffee, the way she'd emptied the beer can. As she put the cup down on the table she looked severely at Nick, like someone acting a schoolteacher. 'You *are* going to take it back, aren't you?'

'Dunno. Suppose so,' Nick said warily.

Leo flipped the wallet open. His fingers went straight to the zip and he pulled out the dwarf and waved it under Nick's nose. 'You ought to be glad of a chance to talk to the kid who owns this. Thought you were an adventure game nut.'

So it was a real set-up. Tailor-made for him. For some reason that made Nick feel much more frightened. 'So what if I am?'

Leaning forward in his chair, one arm round Donna and one arm reaching out for a coffee, Bill spelt it out. 'You take the wallet back and you've got a chance to get on good terms with Joseph Fisher, haven't you? You and he have got a lot in common. Before you know where you are, you'll be into one of those adventure games of yours.' He gave a small, tight grin. 'Out at his house every night of the week, I shouldn't wonder.'

'Oh, come on!' Nick protested. 'Don't you know where Fisher lives? What is it?' He glanced across at the open wallet. '*Holney Seas End.* Only a maniac would think of going out there. It must be beyond Holney and Holney Fen. One of those godforsaken villages out on the Marsh.'

Donna laughed suddenly, like a kind of nervous reflex,

and Bill put a hand on the top of her head. But he didn't take his eyes off Nick.

'If you *don't* go,' he said softly, 'then we're going to think you've stolen this wallet. Aren't we?'

Donna nodded, grinning. 'Have to call the police.'

'But there's only a few coins in it!' Nick said.

Leo stretched, yawning. 'Terrible what some people will do for almost nothing, isn't it?'

'But—' Nick looked round at them all, still hoping it might be a joke. That they would all suddenly roar with laughter at him, for getting steamed up over a wallet with a handful of coppers in it. But no one showed any sign of laughing. Desperately, he turned to Terry.

And Terry smiled. A friendly, encouraging smile. 'Hey, calm down. No one's asking you to cross the polar ice-cap on a camel.'

*No one's asking you* . . . Suddenly the whole thing shifted and Nick saw what Terry was hinting at. They weren't just getting at him. For some reason The Company wanted him to go out to the back end of the Marsh and make friends with a boring kid in the Fifth Year. OK, so things would be nasty if he refused. But if he did what they wanted . . .

'Suppose I do decide to go off and find this kid,' he said, trying not to sound excited. 'When shall I go?'

Bill leaned back, with a small satisfied smile. 'How about now?'

# Chapter 2

Forty minutes later, out in the cold and the half-dark, Nick knew he was lost.

He'd come through Holney and Holney Fen all right, and picked up Holney Seas End on a signpost at a T-junction. (*Four* more miles? The place must be halfway across the North Sea.) But that was the last mention of it. He'd spent ten minutes guessing—right, left, right, left—and then suddenly come to the end.

The road he was on made a last twist and turned into a bumpy track. In front of him was something dark that blocked the way like a great wave, three or four metres high. For a second he thought it was a wall and then he realized that it was further away and bigger. He'd reached the end of everything. The sea bank.

Damn. Damn and damn and double-damn. His bike lights had gone out, because they were on a dynamo, and all he could see was the coarse grass growing at the side of the track and the great shape of the sea bank that shut out any view in front. Nothing for it but to turn round and go back.

Then it struck him that there must be a pretty good view from the top of the bank. Laying his bike down on the track, he scrambled up and looked back over the land.

The wind was bitter, icy and strong, and the Marsh lay spread out in front of him in the vanishing light. Endless unbroken fields, with not a hedge or a tree to break the sweep. Nothing except the drainage ditches and a few odd houses.

The Marsh always sent shudders down his spine. They said the land still shifted, because it hadn't been drained for long and it was still settling. Still treacherous. For a second, in the wind and the gathering dark, Nick wondered what he would do if it suddenly gaped open under him. Then he pushed the idea out of his mind and made himself concentrate.

To the right, about a mile away, was a small cluster of

lighted houses. Great. Except that there was another small cluster on the left, about the same distance away. He screwed up his eyes and tried to remember the turns he had taken, to see where he might have gone wrong, but it was impossible. And all the time it was getting darker and darker and the wind off the sea was slashing at the back of his neck.

Suddenly he heard a whistle from behind him, from the rough ground that lay between the sea bank and the sea itself. For a second he thought it was some kind of bird, but when it came again it was too long, too shrill. He turned to see what was going on and the wind slapped him in the face, so that he had to struggle to keep his eyes open.

Two figures separated themselves from the darkness. One striding along parallel with the bank, ten metres out, and the other on all fours, racing ahead and bounding back again. A man walking a dog.

Nick yelled and waved, but the wind whipped the words straight back at him. Slipping and slithering, he raced down the far side of the bank and tried to hurry across the rough ground.

It was suicidal. He tripped half a dozen times, caught his feet in ditches and nearly twisted his ankle. Then he fell flat on his face with his hands in a patch of mud. For a couple of minutes he just lay there, cursing out loud into the wind.

The man must have seen him fall, because all at once he was there. Two feet in wellingtons approaching fast, while the dog bounced up and barked loudly. Nick hauled himself out of the ditch and stood up to come face to face with the man.

Only it wasn't a man. It was a girl of seventeen or eighteen in a man's overcoat. She had her shoulders hunched and her long hair tucked into the collar and she was staring at Nick. He gulped for breath, embarrassed, and mumbled his question.

'Can you tell me the way to Holney Seas End?'

But the wind whisked his words away before they reached her, so that she shook her head, without smiling. Not a pretty face. Strong and fierce. He tried again, yelling.

'Holney Seas End!'

9

'Yes.' Her lips moved, but it was impossible to follow the directions in the wind. Grabbing his hand, she started to draw on it with a cold finger, marking out the sea bank and the junctions where he had to turn left, then right, then right again. An invisible map, drawn on his nerve-ends. Nick closed his eyes and concentrated on memorizing the sharp movements of her nail against his skin.

'Got it?' she yelled, at last.

He nodded. Smiled. Then, just to double-check, shouted, 'The Stores? Fishers?'

Her head went up and she gave him a strange, sharp look. The next moment she turned, whistled to the dog and strode off again, hands in pockets, shoulders hunched. Ten metres away, she was nothing but a blacker shape against the half-dark.


Holney Seas End was hardly a village at all. A dozen houses clustered on a bend in the road, with a single street-lamp at the corner and one dead-looking pub. It took Nick a few moments to spot the shop, because it was as dark as everywhere else and the blinds were pulled down over the windows. Oh well, no point in floodlighting the place if no one ever came by to see.

He hunted for a bell to ring. No chance. But it didn't seem right to go poking down the side alley, through the gate, so he banged hard on the door and rattled the letter-box.

After a few seconds, one of the upstairs windows opened and a voice yelled at him.

'Yes?' Sharp, as if he was in a hurry. It was Joseph Fisher all right. Nick gave himself an imaginary gold star for thinking of the right person.

'I've got your wallet. You left it at school.'

'You mean you've come all—' Joseph looked backwards over his shoulder as if he had suddenly heard a noise, shouted 'Wait!' and slammed the window shut.

Great. Really polite. It would serve him right if he came down and found the street empty. But that wasn't exactly easy to arrange, with nowhere else to go. Nick stood in the same place, shivering, until he heard footsteps running fast through the shop, towards the door.

Even then he had to wait another couple of minutes. The place was locked up like the Crown Jewels. Joseph shoved a key into the ordinary lock, halfway up the door, and turned it with a click. Then he had to fumble about at the top of the door-frame, with a bolt or something.

At last there was another click. The door opened and Joseph looked straight at Nick.

'Mitchell,' he said.

'Miller.' It was the same mistake everyone made. Mitchell was the other winger in the fourth-year team.

'Of course. Sorry.' Joseph gave a hurried nod and backed away from the door. 'Look, can you come up? I daren't leave them on their own.'

'OK. If you like.'

The minute Nick was inside, Joseph scrabbled around with the keys again and then shot off through the shop at top speed, while Nick was still wondering who he'd got up there that he couldn't leave. Gerbils? Doddering grand-parents? Lighted firecrackers?

There were no lights on in the shop and Nick followed blindly towards the lit doorway at the end, using his nose on the way. A wet-earth-and-parsnip smell that meant veg-etables. Soap powder. Then a patch of nothing much that must be tins or packets of dry goods. It was easy enough to imagine what the place was like, even in the dark. It was a whatever-it-is-we've-got-it-life-and-soul-of-the-village sort of shop.

Also a 'No Loitering' area, obviously. Joseph was through it, across the store-room at the back, and up the stairs so quickly that Nick was almost running to keep track of him. But he nearly wasn't quick enough. As they got to the top of the stairs, there was a shriek and a loud splash and then someone shouted—a shrill, triumphant voice.

'She's diving! Susie's *diving!*'

Joseph was across the landing in one leap, and Nick followed automatically, with a natural instinct to head for disaster. But while he was still outside the bathroom, looking in, Joseph reached the bath, plunged both hands

11

into the water and hauled out a large, red-faced baby.

There was a second of total silence while she gathered her breath and then—EXPLOSION! She screwed her face up and screamed loudly enough to shatter a crate full of wineglasses. Joseph grabbed an ancient, balding towel and wrapped it round her. Then he sat down on the bathroom stool, holding her against his shoulder.

'Sorry.' Through the noise, he grinned at Nick. 'But you can see I had to be here.'

Nick wondered how he would feel if someone from school came by and found him holding a baby. Cringe. Perhaps it would be best just to drop the wallet into Joseph's lap and make off. Leave the conversation to a better time.

But then the little boy who was still in the bath started up again. 'Susie can't get out *yet*. You promised you'd wash our hair tonight, Joe.'

As far as Nick could see, the kid's hair was dripping wet already, but that didn't stop him setting up a relentless chant, adding to the noise that Susie was making.

'You *promised*, you *promised*, you *promised* . . .'

Joseph didn't look amused. 'Don't be silly, Thomas. Can't you see—?'

'. . . you *promised*, you *promised* . . .' Thomas shut his eyes, opened his mouth and began to scream, on a steady, unbroken note.

Joseph gave another apologetic grin. 'Look here, Miller, do you think you could possibly wash his hair? I did promise and it doesn't take a second. Just lather it up a bit and then use the watering-can to wash it off.'

*Watering-can?* Nick stuck his head round the door to look for one, in case he really had heard right.

'Who's that?' Thomas said.

Joseph stared back, as solemn as an owl. 'That's Nick Miller, from my school. If you're nice to him, he might wash your hair.'

Nick stepped into the bathroom, walking carefully on the bare, splintering floorboards, and grabbed the plastic watering-can from the side of the bath.

'I want bubbles,' Thomas said suspiciously. 'Can he do bubbles, Joe?'

'Of course I can do bubbles. I do the best bubbles on the East Coast.' Nick took a quick look around, but there was no sign of a shampoo bottle. 'What shall I use?'

Joseph reached across and handed him the bar of soap from the basin. 'Here.'

'*This?*'

It wasn't even a real bar of soap. It was made of lots of little leftover bits stuck together, lumpy and a bit slimy. Nick didn't fancy touching it, much less using it to wash someone's hair.

Then he remembered that he was trying to get on good terms with Fisher, so he smiled and grabbed it, making himself ignore the slime. 'OK, here goes. Bubbles.'

Thomas screwed his eyes up tight and waited patiently while Nick struggled to get a decent lather out of the miserable soap. There weren't many bubbles to play with, but if Thomas was disappointed he didn't show it. All he said was, 'Water now, please.'

Nick scooped some out of the bath and held the watering-can high in the air. 'Water-demons approaching, with third-grade enchanted waterspouts. Know any good counter-spells?'

Out of the corner of his eye, he saw Joseph lift his head.

'Here come the waterspouts!' Nick said, with relish. 'Bombs away!'

Thomas liked that, all right. He shrieked and spluttered under the water and shouted, 'Bombs!' and 'Crash! Bang!', while Joseph kept very quiet and did clever things with a nappy and a couple of pins—like something out of a cartoon. Surely everyone used disposable nappies now?

When the baby was bundled up for the night, Joseph sat her on the floor and heaved Thomas out.

'I won't be very long now. Can you hang on a little bit longer?'

*You bet*, Nick thought. He hadn't come all this way just to help bath a couple of kids. Anyway, his socks were sopping wet from the ditch he'd stumbled into and he was dying for a cup of coffee.

'I'll wait downstairs, shall I?'

Joseph nodded and Thomas, who was on his lap,

suddenly sat up straighter, beady-eyed.

'Can I go downstairs too, Joe? And have a toffee?'

'Of course not,' Joseph said. He sounded quite severe. 'They're Ruth's toffees. It would be *stealing* if we took one.'

For crying out loud! Nick pulled a face to himself as he went downstairs. How could you steal a toffee? Talk about nit-picking.

There were three doors at the bottom of the stairs. The one facing him led back the way he'd come, into the shop. The other two were both shut. Quietly he opened the one on the left.

It was a lounge. Of sorts. Saggy old armchairs, dusty carpet and no television. Just a half-empty magazine rack and a couple of shelves of books with names like *A Commentary on St. Luke's Gospel* and *Are you Receiving Me?—Prayers for the Man in the Street.* He didn't fancy waiting there. The place was as cold as the Marsh outside.

The door on the right led into the kitchen, and that was a bit better. The floor was muddy and the cupboards were battered, but at least it was warm. There was a rocking-chair in the far corner and a big Formica-topped table in the middle with a mess of plates and cups on it. And a paper bag.

Wandering across to examine the paper bag, Nick found it was half full of toffees. Ruth's precious, *private* toffees, no doubt. Whoever Ruth was. Pulling another face, he unwrapped two at once and put them into his mouth. Then, as an afterthought, he hid the sweet papers in his pocket.

He had barely finished chewing when Joseph came rattling down the stairs, stopping at the bottom to lock the door that led to the store-room and the shop. Then he came in and grinned at Nick.

'That's got rid of them, thank goodness. Coffee?'

'Wouldn't mind.' Nick moved to sit down and his feet squelched. 'Anywhere I can dry my socks?'

'Help yourself.' Joseph waved a hand at the ancient boiler in the corner. 'I didn't realize the bathroom was that wet.' A joke, deadpan. Suddenly Nick felt more friendly towards him.

'The bathroom would have been a whole lot warmer.' He

14

sat down and began to strip the socks off. 'I had a slight misunderstanding with a ditch, when I was trying to find the way here.'

Joseph stopped, with the kettle in his hand. 'You really came all this way, just to bring back my wallet?'

Nick nodded, and tried not to look too smug. 'I just thought—well, it's pretty annoying to be without your wallet, even for a day.'

Joseph looked at him, looked him straight in the eyes, the way people never do. 'That was kind of you. Very kind,' he said seriously. 'Today is Dad's cash and carry day, when he goes to the bank, and that's the only time he'll drive into town. If you'd just phoned, *I* would have had an extra bike ride.'

Nick glanced away, feeling embarrassed and faintly mean. 'Here.'

He slipped his hand into his pocket, pushed the toffee papers further down, and felt for the plastic surface of the wallet. Deftly, with his forefinger, he pushed the zip halfway open and then pulled the wallet out, with the zip underneath.

'Thanks,' Joseph said, holding out his hand.

It worked exactly as it should have done. As the wallet changed hands, three or four coins fell to the floor. And with them was the little dwarf figure. Now there was no need to confess that he had looked at what was in the wallet. They would just naturally start to talk about adventure games.

'Here,' Nick said. 'I'll give you a hand.'

He bent to pick up the little dwarf figure, but he was too slow. Joseph bent down and snatched it up.

# Chapter 3

For a second they were looking straight into each other's eyes. Joseph's were very steady, and Nick realized, suddenly, that they were willing him to ignore the dwarf, not to say a word about it.

Deliberately, he took no notice. 'You're into role-playing games as well, are you?' he said casually. At least, he hoped it sounded casual.

Joseph turned bright red.

'Go on, tell us.' Why on earth should it be embarrassing? 'Where do you play? Who with? Is there a group out here on the Marsh?'

'I—no, it's nothing like that.' Joseph took a deep breath and seemed to pull himself together. 'There's a—sort of a game—that I play sometimes with my sister Ruth. But it's not—it's not the sort of game you'd be interested in.'

'Try me.'

'No, there's no point. It's just a family thing.'

Nick snorted. 'And Susie and Thomas provide the monsters, I suppose?' He did his world-famous Frankenstein's monster impression, lurching across the kitchen with stiff legs and hunched shoulders.

Joseph spluttered suddenly. 'You know, that's just the way Susie walks. Like a robot monster.'

'I like it.' Nick turned and grinned. 'A giant baby would make a pretty classy monster if you think about it. With venomous dribble that corrodes armour?'

Joseph nodded. 'They shove everything into their mouths, too. Anything they can grab hold of. Imagine that with a mouth the size of a cave.'

'And they give out sudden poisonous smells. Evil gases.'

They were facing each other across the table now, but Nick hardly saw Joseph. He was too busy visualizing the Terror Baby. Inventing monsters was his speciality. He fumbled for the details that would make this one perfect.

Joseph frowned. 'They'd be too easy to fight, though. All that soft skin covered in rompers, and no defence from behind. It would be cheating to give them armour.'

Nick thought. 'How about surrounding them with a force field that repels weapons?'

'*Boring.*' Joseph shook his head. 'There's got to be something better than that.'

'I know! I've got it!' Nick banged his hand down on the table, rattling the dirty tea-things piled all over it. '*Noise* warfare. They shriek at a million decibels and the vibrations shake armour to pieces. *And* you get temporarily deafened, so your alertness is reduced for three rounds.'

He liked it. He really liked it. He was so pleased that he laughed at Joseph across the table. And Joseph caught the mood exactly and laughed back at him as he added his own last touch.

'And how about this? Female characters have a psychological prohibition against hurting them. So they lose their turn in the first round of the combat.'

'That's fantastic! Really sexist!' Nick was laughing so much that he could hardly speak. And Joseph was almost choking.

'Ruth would go berserk!'

'Oh, come on! You've *got* to let me in on your game. It would be fantastic.'

The words came out by themselves, and the moment they were spoken Nick felt cold. Because now he'd asked straight out, and he'd have to take the answer he got. Suddenly he knew that he would mind very much if Joseph said, *Push off. Forget it.*

But he didn't. He stopped laughing and looked very solemn, but he didn't say no. 'It's not just my game. There's Ruth as well.'

'Look, is that all? You can't play properly with just two, you know. *Ask* her. Say how great it would be if I joined in.'

'I—'

'There's no harm in *asking.* Where is she, anyway?'

'She's taken the dog out. She'll be back in time to help unload the stuff from the cash and carry. But—'

It was frustrating. Joseph liked the idea—Nick could see

17

he liked it—but there didn't seem to be any way of pushing him over the last little hurdle, to make him agree to ask Ruth.

The kettle boiled suddenly, and Joseph used the excuse to turn away and make the coffee. Nick bit his tongue to stop himself pushing things any more. Wait. That was the best thing he could do. If he hung around until Ruth came in, he could ask her himself. He was good with kids, especially kid sisters. Talk to them as if they were real people, and you could have them eating out of your hand in two minutes.

They sat and drank their weak, pale grey coffee and talked about school and football—nothing talk—while they watched Nick's socks steaming on the boiler.

He ought to have felt good. He'd got himself well in— just as he'd been told to—and he'd found out about the game. But he was all jitters.

Suppose he fluffed it now? Suppose Ruth came in and said, *Let a stranger into our precious, private game? You must be mad, Joseph Fisher!* What would he do then?

What would Terry and the others say?

He pushed his hands deep into his pockets and wrapped the toffee papers round his fingers, first one way and then the other. *I've got to do it. I've got to get into their game.*

There was the sound of an engine and through the window he saw an estate car pull into the yard at the back of the shop.

'That's Mum and Dad,' Joseph said.

*Damn,* thought Nick. But before the car had properly stopped, the kitchen door was suddenly flung open and a big dog bounded into the room.

Ruth followed him, shaking her hair free from the collar of her heavy overcoat. Thick, red hair, twisted into cruel, tight plaits with elastic bands round the ends. Nick was almost too embarrassed to look at her face. He should have guessed, of course. She was the girl he had met out by the sea bank, on the saltings. But she didn't give any sign that she had recognized him. Slipping off her coat, she turned to hang it on the back of the kitchen door.

*Now,* thought Nick. *I've got to ask her about it now.* But

18

he couldn't have got the words out, even if he'd been able to think of any. He had no idea how to start a conversation with someone like that.

It was Joseph who brought the subject up. He did it abruptly, without any of the lead-in that Nick would have used.

'This is Nick Miller, from my school. We've been talking about role-playing games.'

Ruth turned round. 'Yes?' Not exactly cheering.

Joseph persevered. 'He wants to join in.' He paused, as if he expected some reply, but Ruth didn't give him any help. 'To play Jezebel.'

Ruth's face went completely blank and Nick started to panic. The whole thing was going to be over before he'd got a word out. And however was he going to explain that? He could almost see the way Bill would look at him, and hear Donna's sharp, sarcastic voice: *So what did you say to her?*

'It's much better playing with more than two,' he broke in desperately. 'If you haven't played it like that, you won't be able to believe how much better it is.'

'Oh, yes?' Ruth said, very chilly, as if he was trampling over her private ground.

Nick started to get annoyed. What did she know about it anyway, with her fiddling little homemade game? He stopped trying to sound polite.

'You're not really playing at all with only one adventurer. It's when you get a group that people really get into their characters. They begin to argue for what they want. Work out different ways of doing things. Interact. That's when it gets really *testing*.'

Ruth's eyes swivelled towards him, quickly, and for the first time he saw a flicker of interest. As though he had actually said something that made sense to her. He fought the instinct to look away and gave her back stare for stare. One more push. That was all she needed. Then she might really start to wonder about letting him in.

'I'm not saying I could teach you anything,' he said carefully. 'You're the only ones who know how your game works. It's just that having a new player opens up all sorts of—possibilities.'

Ruth nodded slowly. 'Perhaps. I'll have to think about it, won't I?'

That was all. No smile. Immediately she turned away, with the dog leaping after her, and began to climb the stairs.

Nick took a long, deep breath. That was it, then. He had done all he could and now he would have to wait and cross his fingers. Perhaps Joseph would keep up the pressure when he'd gone.

He turned to suggest it, but before he could say anything, the kitchen door opened again and Mr and Mrs Fisher staggered in, each humping a heavy cardboard box. They were both thin and shabby, dressed in old, baggy jumpers and trousers that *his* mum and dad wouldn't have been seen dead in.

Nick didn't expect them to take any notice of him—why should he and Joseph's parents be interested in each other?—but Joseph launched straight into the polite bit.

'Mum. Dad. This is Nick Miller from school.'

Nick produced a nod and a smile, but Mr and Mrs Fisher made a meal of things. Put down their boxes and grabbed hold of his hand, one after the other, to shake it. As if finding him there was some sort of special occasion.

It was all too much. As soon as they let go of him, Nick reached for his socks.

'I think I'd better be getting home.'

Joseph looked at him. 'Sure you can find the way?'

'I wouldn't mind a few directions,' Nick said, as he pulled the socks on. 'I don't fancy finding myself up by the sea bank again.'

'I'll draw you a map. It's not too difficult really.' Joseph rummaged in a drawer for some paper. 'Look, this is the *old* sea bank . . .' His pen flicked over the white surface, making quick neat lines, dividing up the chaos of the Marsh into roads and fields and landmarks that Nick could find, even in the dark.

And all the time, as he watched the drawing and listened to what Joseph said, Nick was thinking that it took practice to be able to draw a map that quickly. What was it that he usually drew? Dungeons? Castle rooms? Forests? . . .

Suddenly he was really curious.

As he cycled back, in the dark and the drizzle, he hoped that Bill and the others would have gone home. It would have been fine to come back, look them straight in the eye, and say: *I've done what you wanted. Mission accomplished.* That would have made him feel like one of them. Leo would have given him one of his big warm smiles, and he might even have got a quick grin from Donna. But as it was, he had no answer at all, and he didn't want to see them until he had.

He was out of luck.

They were waiting by their bikes, under the street lamp, chatting to Terry. No one looked round as Nick cycled up the road, but he could feel them listening.

'Hi,' Donna said as he drew into the kerb. She turned slowly and gave him a long stare, playing it super-cool, until Leo tweaked her hair.

'Have a good ride?' said Bill.

They were teasing him. Pretending they didn't care where he'd been or how he'd got on. But the moment he tried to slide past, Terry's hand was on his shoulder.

'You were a long time,' he said.

'It's a long way.' Nick tried to sound as cool as the rest of them.

'Mum's going crazy in there.' Terry grinned. 'We told her you'd gone out on the Marsh, and she's been having visions of getting a ransom note from that gang.'

Donna laughed again—her nervous bark of a laugh—and Leo put his arm round her throat.

'Unfeeling woman! Have you no pity for Terry's little brother? Out on the Marsh, totally *surrounded* by gangs of vandals, like a little waif in the middle of a gang of Millwall supporters, without his big brother to—'

'Knock it off,' Bill said.

Leo stopped and they all looked at Nick.

'So?' said Bill.

It ought to have been simple. He just had to say, *I asked to join in Joseph's game, and he wants me to, but we have to wait and see what his big sister says.* But if he said that, they'd just write him off as a stupid little kid, too young to join in with anything.

21

'I got on OK with Fisher,' he muttered. 'Like you said, we've got a lot in common. I think we'll get something going.'

'Made a new friend for life, have you?' Bill chuckled suddenly, a dry, creaky chuckle. 'OK, kid, let us know how you get on. You coming, Don?'

Donna shrugged—which meant yes—and straddled her own bike. For a second Nick thought she was going to ask him some more questions, but then the engine roared and she was off up the road, ahead of Bill and Leo.

As the noise died away, Terry looked at Nick. 'They won't forget about it, you know.' He sounded kind. Almost anxious. 'Sure you can handle it?'

'I'm not a baby,' said Nick. 'What's it all about, anyway?'

'All what?' Terry opened his eyes wide, innocently. 'You been getting ideas in your head?'

In other words, loyalty to The Company came before loyalty to any little brother. Nick wasn't quarrelling with the idea, but he hated being shut out. He glanced away.

'What's for tea?'

Terry stopped looking anxious and grinned evilly. '*Coq au vin*. But you don't think you're getting any tea, do you? Not after what Mum's been through worrying about you.'

Nick managed a weak grin in reply. 'You just wait till I start making myself a fry-up on her beautiful new hob. She'll be rushing my *coq au vin* into the microwave.'

He went in to face her. Once he'd done that, he would be able to forget the whole strange business, at least until after half term.

# Chapter 4

But there wasn't any chance to forget, because The Company virtually moved into the house over half term.

It was all the fault of his dad's grandiose plans for the barbecue. Mr Miller came back the next day, after a wildly successful selling trip, and he brought a new barbecue with him. It was three times the size of the old one.

'*Now* we can do things properly!' he said, as he set it up in the lounge, to show it off. 'We're not going to spend *this* barbecue messing about with fiddling little sausages and bits of steak like postcards. We'll have Chinese spare-ribs—kebabs—tandoori chicken—T-bone steaks—'

Nick and Terry looked at each other. That was typical of Dad. He always had to do things better than everyone else.

'Not all on the same evening,' Mrs Miller said faintly. She stared at the gleaming-new barbecue standing beside the cocktail bar as if it mesmerized her.

'Why not?' Mr Miller's eyes gleamed. 'We'll ask the neighbours and the people from the club and all the kids' friends. Make it a really big do.'

Mrs Miller looked as if she was going to pass out. She liked to have everything under control, and Nick could see that she was wondering how to cope. 'But that's such a lot of people. And it's not just the meat. They'd expect all the other bits as well. Salad and relishes and—'

'So? Get the kids to take care of that.' Mr Miller turned to Terry and Nick. 'Your friends will come in and chop things up and do a bit of shopping for your mum, won't they?'

'I reckon.' Terry shrugged.

Mrs Miller smiled feebly. Nick suspected she was a bit afraid of Terry's friends. 'They're such nice boys,' she said. That didn't include Donna, of course, but even Mr Miller preferred to ignore Donna, and her police record.

So The Company took over. For the rest of the weekend,

Nick couldn't go anywhere in the house without finding one or two of them lounging about swigging beer or coffee. They did a bit of work, but mostly they ate and drank and watched Nick. And the more uncomfortable it made him, the more they grinned.

The evening of the actual barbecue was worst, because Livingstone and Parker were there as well.

'It's funny, Livingstone,' Parker said—with a spare-rib in one hand and a chicken joint in the other—'your sister keeps smiling at Nick. D'you think she fancies him?'

'Dunno.' Livingstone eyed Nick. 'You want to be careful, Miller. I can see Bill watching you.'

There was no way Nick could explain. Livingstone might be in on The Company's plan, whatever it was. But he might not. And no one sane would trust Parker with a secret. All he could do was avoid them as much as possible and pretend it wasn't happening.

He escaped to the barbecue. By the end of the evening, he was almost as good at barbecuing as his dad was, but he had terrible indigestion and he never wanted to see another steak or chop or spare-rib in his life.

And even then, The Company didn't go away. They kindly came back the next day, to help clear up—and eat up all the left-overs. Nick gritted his teeth and stuck it out, making himself smile back every time anyone smiled at him.

Soon it would be school again. Then at least he would find out what Ruth had said about letting him into the game. That would settle the waiting, one way or the other.

He didn't have to hang on for long. On the first day after half term, Joseph came up while Nick was still in the cycle shed padlocking his bike.

'Here, Miller, I've brought you some things to look at.'

Livingstone and Parker stopped yacking in the corner and turned round to eavesdrop, not making any pretence about it. Joseph's voice dropped to a mumble.

'Go on, take it.'

He was holding out a plastic carrier bag. Automatically,

Nick took it and peered inside, at the sealed envelope and the two exercise books, battered and furry round the edges.

'What is it?'

'Just a few bits I thought you'd like to see. If you're still interested in—'

Nick got it then, without needing to hear the end of the sentence. 'The game?'

Livingstone and Parker looked at each other and took a step nearer, but Joseph was already going. Nick had to call after him.

'You mean she said yes?'

'There's a note in the bag.' Joseph waved a hand and loped off and instantly Livingstone and Parker were there, peering into the bag and talking in purposely loud voices.

'What's up, Miller? Didn't know you were friends with Holy Fisher.' Livingstone's thin lips were smiling, but he gave Nick a hard look.

'Perhaps he's going to join the Christian Union.' That was Parker, prancing about like an idiot, as usual, and patting Nick's head.

Normally, Nick would have joined in with relish, but today they just annoyed him. He could see Joseph walking away, very upright as if he was having to work to ignore the shouts.

'Knock it off,' he snapped irritably. 'Think there's nothing to life except football and dirty postcards?'

That was *it*, of course. Livingstone gave a jeer of triumph and Parker chanted 'Holy, holy, holy,' all the way into school.


He didn't have a chance to get rid of them all day. Every time they went into a new lesson, they sat down, one on each side of him. They peered into his bag as he got his books out, flicked notes across the geography room—*Let's have a look at your prezzie from Fisher*—and told Sarah Hull, their form prefect, that he wanted to read the next lesson in Assembly. Nick's friendship with Joseph Fisher turned into the Class Joke of the Day.

He managed to keep them off Joseph's stuff by shoving it

underneath all his other things and keeping a tight grip on his bag, but that meant he couldn't look at it himself, and he was burning up with curiosity.

It was the only thing on his mind when he walked in through the kitchen door after school. He grabbed up one of his mother's special ginger flapjacks, aimed a kiss at her left ear—because she liked that sort of thing—and disappeared straight up to his bedroom. Shutting the door, he tipped out the contents of the plastic bag on to his bed. Yes. There were two exercise books and an envelope.

Not quite knowing what to expect, Nick opened the cover of the first exercise book. Rules? Lists of characters? Spells? Weapon ratings and combat tables? There were dozens of things he could imagine.

But it was none of those. The first page was done out like an illuminated manuscript, with neat square black letters in the centre and bright little coloured pictures round the edges, twined into the branches of fantastic, tangled plants. Pretty-pretty stuff.

Except that, when he looked closely, he saw that the pictures were all of monsters. Snake-headed or hump-backed or terribly fanged. Growling and snapping and raking each other with purple claws that left gashes an eighth of an inch long, adorned with drops of crimson blood. The only recognizable animals were at the top of the page. A line of grinning dogs, with wide mouths and blood-stained teeth.

Nick shuddered and began to read the words written in the middle of the page.

> Jezebel, Queen of Darkness,
> we summon you, by the power of the dog.
> Appear before us,
> not veiling your terrible face.
> In the strength of faith,
> we dare to adventure in your kingdom,
> risking all trials,
> and facing all knowledge.
> Appear, O Queen, we charge you.

He read it three times before he took it in properly. It didn't seem to have any connection with the kind of adventure game he knew. For a second he shivered, wondering what he would find when he turned the page.

But when he did, he saw things he understood. *Spell to Detect Magic in a Room. Spell of Invisibility (one round). Spell to Counter Poison.* Pages of spells, followed by lists of weapons. They'd need time to work through. He shut the book and flipped the other one open.

The first book had been carefully written and decorated with little sketches—although no other pages were as elaborate as the first one. The second book was severely practical. Obviously the one that Joseph used while he was actually playing. There were dungeon plans, drawn out step by step as the adventure proceeded, with little notes to remind the adventurer of things:

> Five goblins here with scimitars, all put to flight.
> A dragon on his hoard. Put to sleep by singing.
> Signs of orcs seen.

The maps had unexplored tunnels, blank spaces and question marks. And in one or two places, Joseph had started drawing too far over to the side, so that he'd had to copy the whole thing out and start all over again. But in spite of that, the maps were neat, drawn with the same small, careful black lines as the map of the Marsh that he had made for Nick, quite different from the kind of scrawls that Nick remembered making himself, when he was playing with the school club.

Half the book was filled with dungeon plans, all neatly dated. It looked as though Joseph and Ruth must play almost every day, and as far as Nick could tell, Ruth was always the Game Master. There was no sign that Joseph ever invented dungeons of his own. That was interesting, as well. It all came out of *Ruth's* head?

But what was the Jezebel stuff about? There weren't any clues. The only other thing in the second book was a chart at the back.

| | |
|---|---|
| *Name:* | Jethro the Adventurer |
| *Strength:* | ~~11~~ ~~13~~ ~~12~~ ~~11~~ 12 |
| *Bravery:* | 14 |
| *Intelligence:* | ~~10~~ 9 |
| *Virtue:* | ~~7~~ ~~8~~ ~~9~~ ~~10~~ ~~8~~ ~~9~~ 11 |
| *Faith:* | ~~7~~ ~~8~~ ~~7~~ ~~8~~ ~~7~~ ~~8~~ 7 |
| *Endurance:* | ~~12~~ ~~13~~ ~~12~~ ~~13~~ ~~12~~ 13 |

*Equipment:* sword and shield, six metres of rope, a torch.

Nick wasn't familiar with all the categories, but he'd drawn out plenty of tables like that for his own characters, and he knew what this one meant. Joseph and Ruth settled the fights in their games with dice, the way he was used to, and the numbers in the table were for multiplying the scores of the dice. The exact details of how they did it weren't important—he could easily pick those up. The important thing was that this was the kind of game he knew about, that he had been looking for. He felt suddenly very cheerful as he opened the envelope that Joseph had sent.

> I can't give you much to introduce you to the game— it's mostly in our heads, of course. But I think Ruth is prepared to give it a try with three people, so it might be a good idea if you had a look at these. They're only mine, of course. Ruth's, naturally, are top secret. Feel free to read everything, but please keep it to yourself. (I'd like them back soon, of course.)
>
> If you still want to play, give me a ring (Hol. 5768) and we'll fix a day. Any evening is fine for us, except Tuesday. (Not even the little ones escape the weekly visit to Gran's.)
>
> Joe.

Nick sat on his bed, surrounded by the things Joseph had sent, and tried to work it all out. But before he could make any sense of it, his bedroom door banged open and Terry lounged in.

He picked up Nick's new calculator and pressed a few buttons. 'Dad buy you this? Thought you'd got one already.'

Nick shrugged. 'He met a man in a pub who was selling them cheap.'

'It's not as good as that Casio of Bill's.' Terry turned it over in his hands then dropped it on to a pile of magazines and wandered on.

When he got to the chest of drawers, he picked up Nick's Star Warrior and turned the little figure upside down to examine the painting. 'I hear you've been talking to Joseph Fisher again.'

How did he know that? Livingstone? 'What about it?'

'Going to start up a fearless, heroic game with him, are you?' Terry said, still with his back turned. 'Deadly monsters and heroes going out on daft quests?'

It was meant to be a taunt, but he said it too quickly, too nervously. As if it was leading up to something else.

'Played yourself, have you?' Nick said. 'Know what it's all about?'

'You've got to be joking! It's kids' stuff. I like my danger real, baby brother.'

'That's idiotic,' Nick said. 'Are you going to put your head in a *real* lion's mouth? Fight with *real* swords? Oh, come *on*. Role-playing games let you work out that kind of thing without starting your own war.' He struggled to explain what he felt. 'They're—they're almost a preparation for real things.'

'Oh, yeah? Like *quests?*' Terry laughed. 'Ever know a real person go on a quest?'

'But that's just it. People hunt for things all the time.' Nick's tongue almost fell over itself, he was so keen to explain. 'Things they want to know, exams they need, jobs. Why don't you wake up and look around you. It's what life's all *about*.'

'It is?' Terry turned round suddenly and grinned. 'So you fancy yourself on a real quest, do you? Sir Nicholas the Stainless Hero?'

Nick almost held his breath. 'Try me.'

Terry smiled again. Not wide. Very slow. 'You reckon? Put money on it, would you?'

'Ten pounds,' Nick said. Not riches, but enough to show he was serious.

'You're on.' Terry turned and flicked through the stuff on Nick's desk until he found a piece of paper and a pen.

29

Then he leaned forward and scribbled for a moment or two, shielding the paper with his body. When he straightened, the piece of paper was between his fingers, folded small.

Nick held out his hand.

'Not yet,' Terry said, and held the paper higher. 'Got to have *rules* on a *quest*, haven't you?'

Nick ignored the mocking voice and nodded. 'OK, what are the rules?' It all felt like some kind of game.

'Rule One,' Terry said. 'There's three bits to this quest. You've got to get the lot, otherwise I win. Agreed?'

'Agreed.'

'Rule Two.' He watched Nick hard. 'You can't read this yet. You're to keep it sealed up until the right moment. Agreed?'

Nick shrugged. 'I can't see why, but all right. Stick it down if you're fussed. There's some Sellotape on the desk.'

Terry reached for the Sellotape, broke off a bit and stuck it over the open end of the paper. Then he drew a line right across the Sellotape, so that Nick had no chance of opening it and then sticking it up again. 'Here you are.'

Nick took the folded paper and looked down at it. 'So when *do* I open it?'

Very slowly, Terry turned to the bed. He stared down for a second at the open exercise books and the letter from Joseph. 'You can open it after you've played your game with Fisher for the first time. Not before.'

'OK.' Nick shrugged. 'If that's what you want.'

'And I bet you chicken out when you read it.' But it was a joke, not a taunt, and Terry grinned as he said it.

Then he was through the door and gone. Nick took a long deep breath. 'Bet I *don't* chicken,' he said out loud.

It was all like a game set up ready to play, waiting for someone to make the first moves. Oh sure, he could open the bit of paper and read it straight away, but that would have been it. End of quest. Once you've broken the rules, there's no game any more.

Nick closed his eyes and for a second he could almost see the faces of The Company clustered together in the glare of the headlamps. Could almost hear the voices that muttered beneath the noise of the engines. But this time he didn't feel left out.

He put the sealed paper on his chest of drawers and ran down the stairs to the hall, to telephone Joseph. To set the double game going.

# Chapter 5

On Monday, after school, Nick cycled out to Holney Seas End for the second time.

The shop was already shut when he got there, and it seemed more sensible to go round the side to the kitchen door and knock there. When Mrs Fisher opened it, she smiled so brightly at him that he thought she'd muddled him up with someone else.

'I was here last week,' he said. 'I've come to see Joseph.' He could see, looking past her, that they were all at the table, but the meal seemed to be over.

'We've all been looking forward to seeing you again, Nick,' Mrs Fisher said, as if he'd come visiting the whole family. As she stepped back to let him in, a joyful voice yelled from the kitchen behind her.

'Miller! Millermillermiller! More water-bombs!'

Kids, thought Nick. Put on a show for them one day and they expected something special every time you appeared. He leered over Mrs Fisher's shoulder and bared his teeth. Thomas shrieked with pleasure, Susie giggled and wriggled and Joseph and Mr Fisher waved from their places at the table. Even Ruth managed a small smile.

It was like being a long-lost cousin. Joseph got him a chair, Ruth fetched a plate and cut a slice of cake and Thomas and Susie kept up a constant stream of talk and giggles. It was amazing. As if he was someone special, instead of just a kid from school who'd dropped in for the evening.

Mr Fisher took Nick's hand, as he sat down next to him, and shook it hard. 'It's good to see you here again, Nicholas. It takes a real friend to come visiting this far out.'

For a second, Nick was embarrassed. Then Mr Fisher smiled and he realized that it wasn't just over-polite conversation. The man was really grateful that someone had bothered to come out to the back of beyond.

'Oh, I enjoy coming here,' Nick said airily. 'It's an adventure, like travelling to the end of the world.'

Mrs Fisher gave a quick, tight smile, as if that wasn't such a joke after all, and Nick wondered if he'd been rude. He tried to patch it up.

'It's very peaceful out here. Better than where I live, with motorbikes and things going past in the middle of the night. Nothing like that to bother you out here.'

'Nothing to bother us at all, is there?' Ruth said sharply. 'Makes you long for a bit of excitement, like a few idiots on motorbikes.'

Suddenly, Nick remembered what Terry had said, the first time he came back from Holney Seas End, about Mum being worried. Snippets came back to him that he'd read in the local paper and heard on the news. That gang of vandals—the ones Mum had fretted about—specialized in shops out on the Marsh. He stared down at his plate, uncomfortably.

Joseph got him out of that awkwardness, with a friendly grin. 'It's a long slog cycling in to school, I can tell you.'

Nick pushed the gang to the back of his mind and made himself grin back. 'You need a ten-gear, super-speed racing bike like mine. Makes the miles fly past. Why don't you get yourself a bike with *wheels* instead of a heap of old scrap-iron?'

He'd forgotten what Joseph's bike was like. It was just a joke. But Joseph suddenly laughed, too quickly, Ruth glowered at Nick over the teapot, and Mr Fisher gave Joseph a slow, tender smile. If Dad smiled at me like that in public, Nick thought, I'd punch him in the gut.

'Joseph has to put up with a lot of things,' Mr Fisher said. 'Including his decrepit old bike. He's very patient.'

He smiled at Joseph again, as if he'd done something really special, as if he had really scored by putting up with the hassle of going backwards and forwards to school on a heap of old iron. The only time Nick could remember his own father looking at him like that was when he hit his first fifty. But what was so great about what Joseph had done?

Before he could work it out, Mrs Fisher let the dog out and shepherded the little ones upstairs to the bathroom.

Ruth glanced at Joseph.

'Shall I—?'

He nodded. 'We'll clear up down here. We'll be ready by the time you are.'

She stood up and vanished upstairs and Joseph began to clear a space at the table. Mr Fisher had fetched a pile of papers and was waiting to spread them out. Nick recognized the look of them, because his dad had a heap like that at the end of the month. Bills. But this was a massive pile. And as soon as the table was half clear, Mr Fisher hunched over them, frowning. Joseph started to carry the rest of the dirty dishes over to the sink.

'I'll give you a hand,' Nick said, picking up a pile. He imagined what his mother would have said about the thick, chipped crockery and the mess Susie had made all over the table. But Joseph just grinned and held out the drying-up cloth.

'Ruth's not skiving,' he said. He glanced over his shoulder, at his father, but Mr Fisher was too busy with the bills to notice anything else. Joseph lowered his voice. 'She's gone to get ready for the game. She—' He looked sideways at Nick. 'I don't know what you're expecting, but we've got our own way of playing. You may find it a bit—strange.'

'That's OK,' Nick said. 'Ruth's happy for me to join the game, is she?'

'She was pleased.' Joseph sounded surprised. 'I think she—well, the game's very important to her, and I think she must have got bored, playing with just me. She said—'

He broke off.

'No, tell me.' Nick grabbed a couple of plates and rubbed vigorously at them. '*What* did she say?'

'She said, *It'll be good having a new person. A real challenge.*'

So he was a challenge, was he? Nick felt a quick, unnerving stab of excitement. Well, she wasn't going to find him an *easy* challenge. 'So tell me a bit about the game. How does it work?'

Joseph shook his head and grinned. 'Wait and see,' he muttered.

And that was it. However many times Nick tried to steer the conversation that way, Joseph turned it back to other, more ordinary subjects, until the last cup was dried and stacked away in the cupboard. Then he hung the drying-up cloth tidily over the boiler.

'We're off upstairs now, Dad.'

No answer. Just a grunt.

Joseph led the way and Nick followed, thinking that he hadn't got a clue what was going to happen. Because—what had Ruth been getting ready? There *wasn't* anything to get ready for a role-playing game. A few dice. Notes about the adventure, ready prepared. Some tables about dice-throwing. Nothing else.

Screams and splashes were coming from the bathroom at the top of the stairs. Joseph ignored those and walked along to the end of the landing, to the only closed door. Rattling his fingernails against the wood, he called, 'Ready?'

'Ready.' Ruth's voice from inside the room sounded much further away than Nick would have expected. Distant and muffled. Joseph pushed the door open and they went in.

It wasn't a big room, and it looked smaller because of the large wardrobe at one end. It was heavy and dark, with carved wood at the sides and a mirror on the door. Apart from that, there was a bed, an upright chair by the window and a wooden stool. Nothing else.

And no sign of Ruth.

Joseph pointed across at the bed. 'We'll both sit on that.' He slid the stool across in front of Nick, like a table. 'OK?'

'But Ruth isn't—' Nick glanced round the room, frowning.

Then he realized that Ruth *was* there. Or someone was. He could see four fingers, with scarlet-painted nails, gripping the edge of the wardrobe door, holding it shut from inside.

That was all he had time to notice. Suddenly, Joseph flicked the light switch off. The room was completely dark, except for the strip of night sky, six inches wide, that showed where the curtains didn't quite meet.

The bed creaked as Joseph sat down beside Nick. 'Ready?' he said.

How can you be ready when you don't know what's coming? 'Ready,' Nick said.

'Then I'll begin the invocation,' said Joseph.

He started to chant. It was solemn, almost mechanical, like the voice of some ancient high priest, and he was chanting the invocation from the exercise book.

'Jezebel, Queen of Darkness,
we summon you, by the power of the dog.
Appear before us,
not veiling your terrible face.
In the strength of faith,
we dare to adventure in your kingdom . . .'

Nick's eyes were slowly adjusting to the darkness. He could see Joseph as a black shape next to him, and he could make out the outlines of the wardrobe and the chair in front of the window. But there was no movement, and no sound except Joseph's chanting voice.

He raised it a notch.

'. . . risking all trials,
and facing all knowledge.
Appear, O Queen, we charge you.'

The wardrobe door creaked as it opened and, for a second, Nick wanted to laugh out loud. This wasn't what he'd come for. This was just play-acting.

Then, from across the room, he caught the faint, sweet scent of roses, drifting in the air. Gradually it grew stronger, as if it was seeping out of the wardrobe to fill the room. Something rustled, like rich, stiff material, and there was another, louder creak as Ruth stepped out of the wardrobe.

She came slowly across the room, accompanied by the soft swishing of her skirts and the smell of the roses, and all of a sudden, Nick found that he had screwed up his fists and clenched his teeth. Any minute now, Joseph would flick the light on again, to reveal Ruth all tarted up in fancy dress. And that would be *it*, because he would burst out laughing and they'd throw him out.

But there was nothing like that. Just the darkness and the

36

scent and the quiet rustling. She sat down on the chair in front of the window, a dark silhouette against the narrow opening in the curtains. Nick could see that her hair was piled up on her head, looped into high, fantastic shapes, but he couldn't even guess what her expression was like.

She sat for a moment in silence, and then she spoke, in the same hypnotic, chanting voice as Joseph had used.

'Who summoned me?'

It wasn't a child's voice, playing a game. Ruth wasn't a child. Nick's hands clenched tighter and a long, slow shudder ran up his spine.

'We have summoned you to come up from your catacomb,' Joseph said. 'We want to try our strength against your evil powers.'

The low, cruel laugh from across the room had Nick peering through the dark at her, but it was useless. All he could see was her motionless black shape as she answered.

'Do you bring gifts?'

Joseph wriggled, pulling something out of his pocket, and Nick felt him lay it on the stool.

'We bring gifts.'

'*Both* of you?'

Joseph leaned towards Nick. 'Sorry,' he whispered. 'I didn't think of that. Have you got anything you could give? Something small?'

'A coin?' Nick whispered back.

'Of course not.' Joseph sounded quite shocked. 'This is a *game*.'

Nick felt like saying that ten pence wasn't going to bankrupt him, but he bit back the words. Fumbling in his pocket, he found an old conker which he pressed into Joseph's hand. 'Will this do?'

'Fine.' Joseph laid it down on the stool and raised his voice. 'We both bring gifts.'

'Then give your names, so that I shall know who enters.'

Nick hadn't got the slightest desire to laugh now. He was as solemn as the other two, as he listened to Joseph's reply.

'I am Jethro,' Joseph said, with a note of pride in his voice.

Justified pride, Nick thought, remembering the table in

37

the back of the exercise book. Jethro wasn't a bad character to be playing. Strong and brave and even quite bright.

'My companion seeks a name for his adventuring,' Joseph went on. 'What shall he be called?'

'He shall be called Zephaniah.'

Holy caterpillars! Nick wasn't sure he could even spell that one. Still, names weren't that important. The crucial things were the scores for the different qualities. That must be the next thing to be settled.

Ruth's voice came through the darkness, echoing his thought.

'What character has fortune given him?'

'He waits to discover, O Queen.' Joseph nudged Nick and whispered, 'Here, take these.'

Dice. Three six-sided dice. Nick felt the shapes as he took them. At the same moment, Ruth spoke again.

'Then let him try his luck.'

# Chapter 6

As Ruth spoke, Joseph took a little torch out of his pocket and turned it on, pointing the beam down at the wooden top of the stool. For a few seconds, Nick was distracted, glancing across the room to try and catch a glimpse of Ruth. But the light blinded him to everything beyond the stool, and her voice came out of even deeper darkness, sounding mocking and brittle.

'Are you strong, Zephaniah?'

Nick rattled the dice in his hands and rolled them on to the stool to find out. Three six-sided dice gave a top score of eighteen, but anything over twelve would be good.

Two threes and a one.

'Seven,' Joseph announced.

Nick leaned sideways to murmur in his ear. 'Look, I can't play with a score like that. Can't I—'

'Ssh!' Joseph hissed.

'Are you brave, then?' said Ruth's voice.

Perhaps it would be all right if he got a decent score for bravery—depending on how they played. Nick shook the dice, held them in his hands for a moment and then rolled.

'Four,' said Joseph.

'But that's crazy.' Nick spoke out loud this time. '*Everyone* fiddles scores like that. You can't play otherwise.'

'In my catacombs you must obey the voice of fate,' Ruth said relentlessly. 'Are you intelligent?'

Nick swallowed. He couldn't go *on* getting such terrible scores. Intelligence would probably qualify him to be a magician or something, instead of a fighter. Not the sort of character that appealed to him, but he could probably manage it.

'Intelligence,' he said aloud, and rolled, shutting his eyes.

Even before he opened them, he knew from Joseph's quick gasp that it was another disaster, but he could hardly believe what he saw when he looked. Three. *Three!*—the lowest score you could possibly get. They were asking him to play a character who was a thick, cowardly weakling. Well, they could just forget about it. If Ruth didn't let him roll again, he was going home.

'Are you good, Zephaniah?' she said, and this time he was certain he could hear a sneer in her voice.

Who the hell cared if he was good? What was the point of being good if you were a dead loss? He grabbed the dice and threw them straight down again.

'*That's* better,' Joseph said. 'Thirteen. At least she won't be able to recruit you for her troops. Only two more to go now.'

'I don't think—' Nick began.

But Ruth ignored his voice. 'And what about faith, Zephaniah? Are you a believer?'

This was insane. Nick grabbed the dice and threw them again. And, for heaven's sake, he got three fives. *Fifteen*, for a lousy, pointless quality like faith. Well, that was it, wasn't it? The whole list of qualities that they used. And what he'd thrown was rubbish.

But he'd forgotten endurance. And Ruth really embroidered the question for that one.

'Can you stand firm through fire and water, Zephaniah? Through torture and mockery and false hopes that shatter around you? Can you bear hunger and thirst, pain and exhaustion and the quarrels that threaten to set companion against companion when your quest seems impossible? How well can you endure?'

'No,' Nick shouted. 'No! I can't endure another minute. You know perfectly well that you've given me an impossible character. If I try to play him, I'll be killed the first time we meet a monster. You can keep your dice and you can keep your game!'

He flung the dice down on to the stool and stood up, intending to storm out of the room. But before he could take a step, he heard Joseph give a loud, startled whistle. Glancing down, he saw that the three dice had fallen with the three sixes uppermost.

'Eighteen,' Joseph said, in an awed voice. 'That must

40

mean you can endure almost anything. It's a fascinating character you've got there, Miller. I'd really like to see how he turns out.'

'And shall we discover?' Ruth said, from the other side of the room. 'Do you accept the character that fate has given you, Zephaniah?'

There was something in her voice, some edge, that made Nick stop and think. After all, he didn't know how their game worked yet. In any normal game, he wouldn't stand a chance with Zephaniah, but this clearly wasn't a normal game. And once he'd stamped out, he'd never find out what it was like.

'I don't know,' he said.

There was a pause, while Ruth considered. Then her skirts rustled again as she stood up.

'You have two days to decide. On Wednesday you will return and tell me whether you wish to enter the cata-combs—or to commit suicide.'

And that was it. She swished across the room, stepped up into the wardrobe and pulled the door shut, leaving nothing behind except a scent in the air.

For a moment Nick thought it might be a trick, a way of pretending that time had passed. Perhaps in a minute she would swish out again, announcing that it was Wednesday and that he must make his decision. But nothing happened.

At last, Joseph got up and switched on the light.

'Is that it?' Nick said.

'Must be. Don't forget that it's different for us as well. But I think she meant what she said. Can you come on Wednesday?'

Nick shrugged. 'Might do. And what if I decide to give up on old Zephaniah and let him commit suicide? Do I get another character?'

Joseph looked doubtfully at him. 'That would be pointless, wouldn't it? You can't do that in real life.'

'But this *isn't* real life! It's only a game, for Christ's sake!'

Joseph didn't exactly wince at the last two words. He gave something more like a startled blink, as though he hadn't expected to hear those words in that place. 'I told you it wasn't the sort of game you were used to playing.'

41

Well thank *you*, Joseph Fisher! There wasn't much point in talking then, was there? Nick glowered and headed for the door. 'I'm off. Don't bother to come down.'

'See you on Wednesday?' Joseph called after him.

'Perhaps. I don't know.' Nick pulled the door shut after him and walked quietly down the stairs, forcing himself not to run.

He should have known better than to get himself mixed up with Joseph Fisher. How could he ever have imagined that the two of them would have anything in common? And as for that crab-faced Ruth, and the two dreary parents . . .

Joseph's parents.

As he reached the bottom stair, their voices stabbed suddenly into his thoughts, coming from the shabby sitting room on the left. What were they up to? Arguing? *His* mum and dad only ever talked like that—on and on and on— when they were having a row.

But the voices didn't sound angry, only very serious. For a second or two, Nick listened to them muttering away, wondering what people found to say to each other after living together all those years.

Then Mrs Fisher raised her voice. 'I've got no *right* to complain,' she said firmly. 'No, I don't like it any better, but I chose to come back.'

'It was my fault you had to come back *here*.' Mr Fisher was almost shouting now, but he still didn't sound angry. More—miserable. Choked.

Then the voices sank to a murmur again and at the same moment, Nick caught sight of himself in the mirror that hung opposite the bottom of the stairs. Saw himself standing, frozen, listening to what was going on behind the closed door. Eavesdropping. Instantly he was terrified that Mr Fisher might come out, that Joseph or Ruth might come downstairs, and catch him snooping.

As if he *cared* what they were up to. All he wanted was to be out of this run-down, depressing house as soon as he could. He was down the last step and into the kitchen before he had taken his next breath.

When he got home, he raced upstairs and flung himself on his bed. What did he do now? Ruth was mad and Joseph was totally under her thumb. Who wanted to play a game with a hopeless character? A loser? There was nothing *to* Zephaniah the way the dice had set him up, none of the exciting, heroic qualities that you needed to be an adventurer.

Grabbing a bit of paper from his desk, Nick began to write down Zephaniah's characteristics, in a sort of frenzy.

| | |
|---|---|
| *Name:* | Zephaniah |
| *Strength:* | 7 |
| *Bravery:* | 4 |
| *Intelligence:* | 3 |
| *Virtue:* | 13 |
| *Faith:* | 15 |
| *Endurance:* | 18 |

Oh, for crying out loud! It was appalling. It was even *worse* than he had thought. Whatever the rules of Ruth's catacombs were, he couldn't believe that he could meet with anything except disaster, with characteristics like that. And even if he was wrong, and those scores meant he could amass a mega-fortune and rule the world—he didn't *want* to be a weedy, scared, moronic saint. He wanted to be strong and brave and clever. If they thought he was going to turn up on Wednesday, they were going to be disappointed.

Crumpling the piece of paper, he threw it at his waste-paper basket, but his rage interfered with his aim. The ball of paper hit the side of the basket and bounced off sideways, to fall under his desk.

As he bent to pick it up, he saw another piece of paper lying under the desk. It must have fallen there when he grabbed at the clean sheet of paper, as he stormed into the room. It was a small, folded bit of paper, stuck up with Sellotape.

The moment he touched it he remembered, amazed that he could ever have forgotten. Terry's note about the quest. To be opened after his first session of playing with Joseph and Ruth. Gently he slid his finger under the Sellotape to loosen it and unfolded the letter. It was short and sweet. Typical Terry style.

Been to Holney Seas End? OK then, hero. Here's—
your quest.
  1. How does the burglar alarm in the shop work?
     (and where are the keys kept?)
  2. Where is the money put when the shop's shut?
  3. When does it go to the bank?
Find them out—if you dare.

For a moment Nick stood still, in the middle of his bedroom, staring down at the paper. In his head he could hear Terry's voice saying, *I bet you chicken out when you read it.* And he could see the eyes of The Company at the barbecue, watching him. Bill and Donna, Terry and Leo, all watching and waiting. But he'd never guessed what they were waiting for. They were asking him—

Without consciously calling it up, he heard Joseph's voice in his head. *If you'd just phoned, I would have had an extra bike ride . . . Today is Dad's cash and carry day, when he goes to the bank.* Wednesday.

For a moment Nick stared at the piece of paper, feeling very cold. Then he crumpled it up, pushed it into his pocket and pulled his maths books out of his school bag. The whole idea was ridiculous. Terry couldn't be serious.

But it wasn't so easy to push the quest to the back of his mind. The list of things he had to discover kept bobbing around in front of his eyes while he was trying to solve equations. And the watching eyes—Bill's and Donna's, Terry's and Leo's—stared up at him from the diagrams in his physics book. Waiting.

He didn't go to bed until late, and it was almost midnight before he fell asleep. Half an hour later, he was woken by the noise of Terry coming back on his bike. He opened his eyes on darkness, to find himself sitting forward, shaken and sweating, listening to the sound of the engine.

That was when he realized how frightened he was.

# Chapter 7

The next morning he was so tired that he could hardly get out of bed. His mum was working an early shift, so she wasn't there to stop him oversleeping, and he got up almost too late and staggered downstairs in a daze. Mr Miller yelled at him as he came into the kitchen.

'Look at you! Your shirt's hanging out, you've got odd socks on, and you haven't brushed your hair. How do you expect to get anywhere in life if you go out looking like that?'

Blearily pushing toast into the toaster, Nick looked at his father's gleaming hair, his shiny, clean, smooth-shaven face, the bright pocket-handkerchief that matched his tie. How did Dad have the *energy* to get up and dress like that every morning? Wasn't he ever miserable, or tired, or worried out of his mind?

'Pull yourself together,' Mr Miller said. 'You don't look fit to go out.'

Nick looked at the clock, gulped down a mouthful of milk, and abandoned his toast. 'I'll be fine, Dad. I've got to go.'

If only he could get to school, he could bury himself in silly jokes and gossip—even in lessons. There would be no time left over to *think*. All he had to do was get there.

He made it as far as the High Street. Halfway along, he had to stop at a red traffic light and as he braked, he heard a voice from the pavement.

'Hi, kid.'

Leo. It took him a second or two to spot him, because he was dressed ready for work, standing in the doorway of the baker's with his white overall on.

Leo beckoned.

'I'm late,' Nick said, looking at his watch.

'For *school*?' It was mocking, amused. 'Come on, I only want a word.'

Nick hesitated and then pushed his bike across the pavement. 'What's the matter?'

'Nothing's the matter.' Leo grinned down at him. 'I just wanted to ask you if you'd read that note of Terry's yet.'

Nick felt sick. He couldn't move, he couldn't think, without someone spying on him. 'So what if I have?'

'Hey, why the tombstone face?' Leo prodded him in the shoulder. 'Come on, kid, it's supposed to be *fun*. A game.'

Did he mean the quest or did he mean what The Company would do after the quest? Nick wasn't sure. Leo acted as though everything was a game. Nick looked down at his feet. 'You lot may be playing a game,' he muttered. 'I feel more like one of the pieces.'

'So—take the game over,' Leo said. 'What do you think we're doing? Me and Terry and the others? We're making everyone play *our* rules for a change.'

'You mean—' Nick began. Then he stopped. If he asked what The Company was up to, Leo might be easy-going enough to tell him. But then he would know, for sure, and suddenly he wasn't at all sure that he wanted to know.

Instead, he snatched the idea he wanted out of what Leo had said. A game. The quest was just a game, for fun. If he played it according to the rules, Leo and the others would keep off his back—and what business of his was it to worry about what happened afterwards?

That blocked out a lot of problems and questions. Grinning at Leo, Nick began to push his bike back to the road. 'Don't worry about me,' he called over his shoulder. 'I'm great at games.'


Games. That was the key word. He muttered it over and over to himself, all day, whenever people stopped talking to him. *Games. Games. It's all a game, to win ten pounds off Terry. I won't be doing any harm, and I'm not responsible for what other people do with what I find out.*

All the same, when he heard Joseph's voice, at the end of afternoon school, he froze for a second, before he could adjust his mind.

'Hey, Miller, how about coming straight back with me after school tomorrow?'

'I—' Nick scrabbled for words.

'We could have something to eat before we play.'

*He knows. He knows I'm thinking of not coming, and he's trying to make it hard for me to cry off.* Nick stood still and turned to stare, to put Joseph on the spot. 'What for?'

'Well—' Joseph wasn't quite meeting his eyes. 'The kids would love it. Thomas has been going on about you ever since Monday, boring us all silly.'

'I might.' Nick was flattered, but he wasn't going to be conned.

Suddenly, Joseph looked straight at him and grinned. 'Oh, go on. It'll be OK, you know. Ruth's not daft. She just wants to let you know she's boss. Once that's sorted out, she'll make sure the game runs all right.'

He grinned again, and suddenly there was a choice. Stop pretending and grin back—or chuck the whole thing in. It was as if they'd been playing a game on the side and Joseph had undercut the whole thing. Nick hesitated.

Before he'd made up his mind which way to jump, Livingstone and Parker came thundering round the corner. When they saw Nick and Joseph standing together, they yelped with delight and Joseph's smile vanished. His face went tight and private.

Just for a second, Nick thought he saw him screw up his fists, as if he longed to punch out at the jeering faces coming towards them. But he surely must have been mistaken. He couldn't imagine Joseph losing his temper. *Joseph?*

Automatically, to break the tension, Nick nodded. 'OK. I'll see you at the bike sheds tomorrow afternoon.'

'Great,' Joseph said. And he was off, heading back into school. For a second Nick watched, wondering which meeting he was staying late for. The boring old debate on the Bomb or the film of wildlife in Borneo. For some reason it annoyed him not to be able to guess.


After school the next day, Nick was on his bike long before Livingstone and Parker had dawdled out of school, cycling

47

out into the Marsh. *Must be crazy*, he thought. He could have been in the warm, eating, but instead he was pedalling away from his comfortable home, with his hands freezing to the handlebars and a cold wind blowing down his neck. Ahead of him, in the fading light, Joseph was rattling along on his ancient bike, at a furious pace.

Well, it was different for him. He did this journey every day, could probably do it in his sleep. He seemed to have gone over to automatic pilot, in fact, because when they reached the shop he made straight for the side gate, as if he had forgotten that Nick was following. He was halfway through before he turned.

'Oh—you might as well bring *your* bike round to the back yard. Out of the way.'

Nick nearly laughed out loud. Out of the way of *what*, for heaven's sake? He was ready to bet that there wouldn't be another vehicle along this bit of road before he left. But he nodded obediently and wheeled his bike past the shop, towards the side gate.

It was the first time he'd been there in any kind of daylight, and he was shaken to see how sad and dingy the shop looked. Faded packets in the window display and cracked and flaking paint round the door. The whole place needed a face-lift. Thoughtfully, he pushed his bike through the gate, past the kitchen door and into the concrete yard at the back.

The yard was almost as depressing as the shop. A swing with a broken seat stood drooping in one corner, and there was a parking space by the double gates that led to the back road.

'Shove it over here, against the shed,' Joseph said, as he leaned his own bike against the rickety wooden wall.

'Fine.' As Nick swung his bike round, he reached in his pocket automatically, to pull out his padlock. Stupid! He shoved the chain back in and the two movements dislodged a stray pound coin. It fell out of his pocket and went rolling towards the back of the house. Before he could put his bike down and grab at it, it had reached the back wall and disappeared.

It must have fallen flat, in shadow. Leaning his bike

48

against the shed, Nick went across to feel for the coin on the ground. And saw the crack. Not a wide crack. An inch, or an inch and a half, maybe, no more. But it ran all along the concrete, close against the back wall of the building.

He was just wriggling his fingers down into it, to see if he could feel the edge of his coin, when Joseph came up beside him.

'Sorry. That's no good. If anything falls down that crack, you have to kiss it goodbye.'

'Jaws of hell?' Nick tried squinting into the narrow darkness. 'How deep is it then?'

'Deep,' Joseph said. His voice had suddenly gone tight. 'It goes right down, through the foundations of the house.'

Nick looked up at him. 'Is that safe?'

'Depends what you mean.' Joseph stared down at the crack. 'The house isn't going to fall down on your head today. But one day it will fall, as the ground shifts.'

'So why don't you mend it? Fill the crack up with concrete . . .?' Nick's voice faded, because he could see the answer to his own question, in the lines of concrete that ran on either side of the crack.

Joseph nodded. 'Never lasts more than six months.'

'Bloody hell,' Nick said. 'I'd sell up and get out if it was me, double quick.'

'Think we don't want to?' Joseph said wryly. 'But who'd buy it—once their surveyor had seen that crack?'

'But—' Surely no one could be caught like that, with no way out. 'What about insurance?'

'*Insurance?* Think anyone'll insure you against shifting? On this bit of the Marsh?' Joseph's voice rose as he spoke, and Nick felt annoyed. What did he think he was? An idiot?

'I bet if you filled it in, really well, you could sell the place before the crack opened up again. I bet no one would guess.'

Joseph looked at him for a moment. Then he said stiffly, 'Perhaps we could, but it wouldn't exactly be honest, would it?'

Nick snorted. 'That's just a cop-out. An easy way not to think about things.'

'You think it's that easy?' Joseph hissed furiously. 'Being

honest about something when you're desperate to get rid of it? You ought to try it yourself sometime, Miller. It's *bloody* difficult!'

For an uncomfortable moment they were glaring at each other, and then Nick snatched at a way to change the subject.

'Hey look, how about this? Suppose we had a potion that shrank us to half an inch high? That crack would make a fantastic dungeon entrance.'

Joseph didn't answer. Just went on staring down into the crack.

'Come on, work it out. Mice ten times as big as us!' Nick shut his eyes to imagine it. Pretty good. 'Ants. Beetles. Oh—and the ground shifts, of course, so you can't quite rely on your map.' That *had* to get him going. It was a winner. 'What about it?'

'It's supposed to be a *fantasy* game,' Joseph said roughly. He stepped past Nick and pushed the kitchen door open. 'We're home!'

Before Nick got his breath back, a shrill voice shouted through the door.

'Miller! Miller!'

Thomas came bombing out and flung himself at Nick, grabbing his trouser-leg with both hands.

Nick growled. 'Where's that baby of yours? I'm feeling hungry.'

Giggle, giggle. Squeal, squeal. Nick let Thomas drag him into the kitchen. Susie was standing up in her playpen, chortling her head off, and Ruth was sitting at the table with the paper in front of her. As soon as Joseph and Nick walked in, she stood up and grabbed her coat.

'OK?'

'OK,' Joseph said. 'Miller and I will give the kids their tea.'

'Great. See you later. Come on, Pickles.'

And that was it. No nonsense about hallo-it's-nice-to-see-you-glad-you-decided-to-come-back-Nick. Ruth was out of the door before he could even smile.

Nick looked across at Joseph. 'Off to the sea bank again, is she?'

Joseph picked up the tin opener and began to open a can of beans. 'Makes a change for her. She hates the shop. Nearly went mad when she had to leave school last year, to help out.'

'So why leave?' Nick picked up a toy dog and began to growl at Susie. 'The shop's not that big.' (Grrrr! Grrrr!) 'Can't your mum and dad manage it by themselves, even with the kids?' (Grrrr! Grrrr!)

'She—' Joseph went red, stuttered to a stop, and then began again. 'Well, if you must know, Mum went off a couple of months after Susie was born.'

'*Your mum?*' Nick was too amazed to be tactful.

Joseph went even redder. 'I don't mean she went off with someone else—it wasn't like that. She just couldn't bear living out here on the edge of nowhere any more.'

'So your dad had the shop *and* the kids.' It didn't exactly take genius to work out what had happened. Nick began to see why Ruth had such a grouch at life. 'But what about when your mum came back?'

'Oh, I dunno.' Joseph shrugged. 'It was all so—there was Mum being guilty about going off, Dad being guilty about living here, both of them being guilty about setting us a bad example. Ruth just went on helping until things got a bit better, and then she somehow seemed too old for school. And the Tech's too far.'

Nick could just imagine it all. Hastily he pushed it to the back of his mind. Looking away from Joseph's face, hunting for something else to talk about, he suddenly realized that there was only one tin of beans.

'We're just feeding the kids now, are we?'

'Afraid not. All together.' Joseph misunderstood his expression, and grinned. 'You should be safe if you sit over the far side of the table. Can you get them some milk out of the fridge?'

Nick opened the fridge door. Joseph was looking pretty competent, heating the beans, laying the table and dealing with the kids, all at once. 'Do you do this often?'

'Every Wednesday, usually, because it's early closing. Mum and Dad are off at the bank and the cash and carry, and Ruth takes the dog.'

51

*Click*, went Nick's mind, filing the information away. Then, idiotically, he was afraid that Joseph would have seen from his face what he was doing. He said something— anything—to change the subject.

'Don't your parents worry about Ruth going out on the saltings on her own? It's pretty lonely out there.'

'Thomas, go and wash your hands.' Joseph pushed him towards the sink. Then he glanced over his shoulder at Nick. 'She's probably safer right out there than she is in the shop.'

'Safer?' Nick didn't pick it up for a moment.

Joseph glanced at Thomas, but Thomas had business of his own with the soap, and he wasn't listening. 'You know. That gang of bikers. The police reckon they come over from Grantham, but they can't catch them. They broke into another shop on Monday night, over at Stanport St. Leonard. Dad said they wrecked the place.'

Nick nodded, slowly. He had looked away uncomfortably when it came on the local news on Tuesday night. And Mum had jumped up and changed channels. She didn't think the gang came from Grantham.

'It's always shops like ours,' Joseph muttered. 'Places where there's not too much money around and where— where it's easy to make people nervous.'

Especially people like Mr and Mrs Fisher, who weren't in very good shape to begin with. People who didn't have enough money to risk losing any of it. Nick didn't want to think about that.

He lifted Susie out of the playpen and put a bib round her neck. 'Up in your chair,' he said to her as Thomas came back, holding out dripping hands. Joseph turned away to find a towel, and then they were all ready for tea.

Hooray. Even if it *was* only toast and beans. That ride in the cold had set his stomach flapping against his ribs. He was just reaching for his knife and fork when Joseph said, 'Thomas. Susannah.'

They shut their eyes—clunk—just like that and, before Nick had even worked out what was happening, Thomas squeaked at Joseph, 'Miller ought to say grace.'

'Ssh!' Joseph said.

'No.' Thomas opened his eyes again. 'I want Miller to say grace. You know Dad always asks visitors. Why don't you—'

Joseph frowned at him. 'That's only when we have visitors from the congregation. It's different. Now will you please—'

'*Why* is it different?' Thomas whined.

Nick looked down at his beans. He could *see* them getting cold, all for the sake of a few lousy words. What did it matter who said grace? He glanced at Joseph. 'I don't mind.'

For a second they stared at each other. Then Joseph nodded. 'OK. If you like.'

No point in hanging about. Nick shut his eyes, bent his head, and gabbled the only grace that he knew. That he thought he knew. 'Lord bless this food to our use and thyselves to our service. Amen.'

There was an odd pause. Then Thomas said, 'That was a funny grace.'

Joseph frowned at him again. 'Come on. Eat your beans.'

Something strange about his voice made Nick run the grace over again in his head, and he realized what he had said . . . *and thyselves to our service* . . . For heaven's sake, it was only a slip of the tongue! There was no need for Joseph to look so po-faced about it. Did he think it had been done on purpose?

Nick started to shovel up his beans as if he hadn't noticed anything wrong, but inside his head he was defending himself, furiously. *It doesn't matter what they think anyway. I'm not moving in. I'm on a quest and they're enemy aliens.*

# Chapter 8

*Half an hour!* That's what it took them to eat their miserable tiny ration of baked beans. Nick finished his in three mouthfuls and sat twiddling his thumbs, wishing he could ram the food down the kids' throats.

But Joseph was maddeningly patient, especially with Susie. *Here comes the little train chuffing into the tunnel . . . One, two, buckle my shoe . . .* There seemed to be a different game for every spoonful. He certainly had no chance of saying anything sensible to Nick. And he did this every week? It was a wonder he could talk reasonably at all.

Left to himself, Nick sat and thought about his quest. How would he go about finding out the other things on the list—if he really intended to do it? They weren't the sort of questions you could ask in a straightforward way. *Where do you keep the takings from the shop? And how about the keys?* Yes, he could just see Joseph's face if he started making remarks like that. It would take a lot of cunning and a lot of nerve to discover the answers—pretty much like winning treasure on a real quest, when he came to think of it.

And then Susie picked up her plate, dumped it upside down on the floor, and began to howl. Joseph looked apologetically at Nick.

'She's had it. Really flaked out. I ought to put her to bed straight away, but it's too early for Thomas. Do you think you could—?'

For one brain-curdling second, Nick thought he was being asked to bath the baby. Then he realized what Joseph meant. 'Oh sure. I can play with Thomas for as long as you like. We can—'

Out of the blue—he hadn't even thought of thinking of it—a stunning idea leapt into his head. Dead clever. *If* it worked. As long as he had the nerve to try it. Nick swallowed the rest of his sentence and grinned at Thomas.

'We'll have a good game, won't we?'

'Yes! Yes, yes, yes! We'll have a super game!' Thomas shrieked.

Nick let him prance about until Joseph and Susie were safely upstairs. Then he beckoned. Thomas came racing up.

'Is it now? Are we going to play the game now?'

His face was eager and bright, and for a second Nick nearly changed his mind. It seemed—somehow—grubby to play the sort of trick he was planning.

'Miller? Can we play now?' Thomas pulled his sleeve.

*Oh, for heaven's sake, it's only a bit of fun. Just to see if I can find the things out. What's the point in getting all serious about it?*

'Yes,' Nick said. 'We're playing now.'

'Hooray!'

'Ssh. It's not a noisy game.'

'No?' Thomas looked disappointed.

'No,' Nick said firmly. 'We're going to be very, very quiet.' He glanced across at the stairs, just to make double sure nobody was listening. 'We're going to play burglars.'

'*Wicked* burglars?'

'*Very* wicked burglars.'

The disappointed expression vanished and a wide grin spread over Thomas's face. 'I'm going to be a very, very, very, very, *very* wicked burglar.'

Ah. That wasn't quite how the plan went. Nick thought quickly. 'Don't you want to be the brave shopkeeper who saves the shop from being robbed?'

'No. I want to be the very, very, very, very, very, *very*—'

'OK, OK.' Nick tried another tack. 'You can be the burglar, and *I'll* be the shopkeeper.'

That went down all right. Thomas chuckled and bounced up and down. All-le-*lu*-ia! At last they could move on. Nick arranged his face into a puzzled frown.

'But you'll have to help me if I'm going to be the shopkeeper, otherwise I'll get it wrong. Because I've never lived in a shop, and I won't know what to do.'

All right, so the story wouldn't have fooled a police cadet on his first morning. But it was good enough for Thomas.

He nodded wisely and looked around.

'Where's the shop?'

'Here.' Nick waved at the table, pushing all the dirty plates out of the way. 'And this is the till.' He picked up his school bag and dumped it on the edge of the table. 'Now, what do I have to do when I shut up the shop for the night?'

Thomas looked round again. 'You have to lock up. Where are the doors?'

'Don't you—' Nick glanced quickly at the stairs and lowered his voice. 'Don't you take the money out of the till before you lock up?'

'You can't do that.' Thomas looked scornfully at him. 'If you take the money away, there won't be anything for me to burgle.'

Damn. Nick forced himself to smile. 'But you can burgle it from wherever I put it, can't you?'

'But then I won't be burgling a *shop*.' Thomas began to frown rebelliously.

'OK, OK.' Better to give in before he made a scene. Perhaps he didn't know, anyway. Nick tried another tack. 'So how do I lock up?'

Thomas wasn't ready to stop arguing. 'But if you lock up, how can I get in to burgle?'

Nick thought fast. 'If I *don't* lock up, you won't be able to batter the door down, will you?'

That was a winner. It took Thomas about a hundredth of a second to agree that he wanted to batter the door down. He liked the idea so much that he moved the game along himself, pointing at the high chair.

'That's the front door. And Joe's chair is the back door. You have to lock them both. The front door is first.' Solemnly, he pulled the high chair to one side and pushed it back into its original position. 'Now it's shut.'

'And locked?' Nick said quickly.

Thomas poked a finger at the high chair. 'Lock, lock. Lock, lock.' Then he stepped back. 'Now you'll have to lift me up, so I can reach the other lock.'

Nick held his breath for a second. Then, very quietly, he said, 'What other lock?'

'For the alarm, of course,' Thomas said impatiently. 'It's

at the top of the door, and I can't reach up there by myself.'

He stretched out his arms and as Nick picked him up he felt squeamish again. Thomas was so small and his bones seemed so fragile. It *was* foul to be conning someone like that. Perhaps he should forget the whole thing.

Then, in his head, he heard Leo saying, *Come on, kid, it's supposed to be fun. A game.* That was it. The whole quest was just a game, a dare, to win ten pounds. Shutting his mind, deliberately, to everything except what he was doing, Nick lifted Thomas towards the top of the chair.

'Lock, lock, LOCK!' Thomas said, enjoying himself. 'Now the other door.'

Obediently, Nick carried him over to the other chair. Thomas locked it up, at the middle and the top, with his outstretched finger. Then he looked at it and giggled, suddenly.

'Can I make the noise when I batter it down?'

Nick didn't think fast enough. 'The noise?'

'When it goes brrrrrrrrrrrr—' Thomas screeched the sound at the top of his voice and began to wriggle around, thrashing with his arms and legs. Hastily, Nick put him down on the ground, but that didn't stop the noise.

'Brrrrrrrrrrrrrrrrrrrrr—'

'OK, Thomas, that's enough.'

'Brrrrrrrrrrrrrrrrrrrrr—'

'Ssh!'

'BrrrrrrrrRRRRRRRRRRRR—'

'THOMAS!' Nick put his hands over his ears and yelled. What did the kid want to do? Turn into an electric bell? 'STOP!'

'Brrrr—' Thomas paused briefly and looked injured. 'How can I stop? You haven't turned me off, have you?'

'How do I do that?'

'BRRRRR—'

'Thomas—'

'BRRRRR—'

It was as bad as a real burglar alarm. Any minute now, Joseph would be calling down the stairs, wondering what was going on. Desperately, Nick risked a guess. He pointed his finger at the top of the high chair and chanted, 'Unlock, unlock, unlock.'

Magic. Thomas stopped at once and gave him a suspicious look. 'Have you got the big key-ring, then?'

'Of course I have.' Nick pretended to jingle the keys at him. 'I'm the shopkeeper, aren't I?'

'And I'm the burglar?'

'That's right.'

Thomas jumped up from the floor. 'I creep into the shop?'

'You do.'

'Break down the door?'

Nick nodded. Unwisely. A huge grin flashed on to Thomas's face.

'And I set off the burglar alarm and it goes brrrrrrrrrr—'

'Thomas, I haven't set it yet.'

'Brrrr—'

'THOMAS!'

Thomas didn't even hear. He was all hyped up, yelling his head off and grinning like crazy as he crashed round and round the kitchen, bumping into the furniture. Nick was just beginning to think he would have to grab him up and throttle him when the back door opened.

'Thomas,' said Ruth, 'stop that.'

It wasn't loud, but it worked immediately. Thomas stopped dead still, closed his mouth, and changed from a raging tornado into a sheepish-looking small boy.

Nick felt pretty sheepish himself and a fraction worried. How much had she heard? 'I was only playing with him. So Joseph could put Susie to bed.'

'That's kind of you,' Ruth said stiffly. 'It's easy to let him get out of hand at this time of night. You have to be calm to keep him under control.'

Under control. Boss Ruth Fisher and her life motto. Nick saw her watching him thoughtfully, eyes narrowed. Thomas wasn't the only one she wanted under control. Well, she wasn't going to get the better of *him*. He tried a bit of polite rebellion.

'He wasn't doing any harm, anyway, were you, Thomas? Just a bit of fun. Self-expression.' That sounded good.

But not to Ruth it didn't. She looked as sour as an old lemon. 'Nothing particularly good about self-expression.

There are some things we're not meant to express.' She turned and yelled up the stairs. 'Aren't you ready for Thomas yet, Joe?'

Joe appeared at the top of the stairs. 'Fine. Send him up. I've just put Susie down and she's gone out like a light.'

Ruth nodded at Thomas and he scampered up the stairs without a word of argument. Nick wondered if he could get away with doing the same thing, but Ruth hadn't finished with him yet. She looked at him hard.

'Have you come to play Jezebel? Or just to fool about with the kids?'

Nick stared back. 'I'm playing.'

She gave a little nod, brisk and sharp, as if he had done what she expected. 'That should be interesting.'

'Yeah, very interesting,' Nick said lightly. He went on staring back and then grinned suddenly, just to see what she would do.

Nothing. All he got was another nod as she turned away towards the kitchen door.

'That sounds like Mum and Dad back from the cash and carry,' she said.

'I'll give you a hand unloading the stuff.'

'Thanks.'

All very polite, but so chilly you could get frost-bite talking to her. Nick stared at her back for a second, wondering what went on in her head.

Then she pushed open the kitchen door, as the estate car pulled up, and he followed her outside to help Mr and Mrs Fisher unload. Suddenly he was impatient for the waiting to be over and the game to begin.

# Chapter 9

'Now,' said Ruth's voice, and Joseph pushed the bedroom door open.

It was dark inside, and a smell of flowers and spice curled out to meet them as they stepped in. Across the room, two tiny points of light glowed dull orange. Incense sticks.

Nick was expecting to go through all the play-acting again, with Joseph chanting the Spell of Summoning and Ruth coming out of the wardrobe. Instead, from Ruth's chair by the window came a faint rustle. She was already there. Nick's muscles tightened, and the adrenalin flooded into his blood. It was like finding yourself in an ambush.

'Over here.' Joseph caught his elbow and piloted him over to the bed. Before they sat down, Nick had banged his shins twice and he had to bite his tongue to stop himself swearing out loud.

Ruth let them sweat it out for a couple of minutes before she spoke. When her voice came, it was cold and formal.

'Jethro. Zephaniah. You are here.'

'We are here.' Joseph switched on his torch and laid it down on the stool. It made a small, concentrated pool of light. Pulling his dwarf figure out of his pocket, Joseph stood it carefully in the middle of the light. Then he nudged Nick.

*Sorry mate,* Nick said inside his head, as he pulled his Star Warrior out of his pocket. *You're stuck with being a feeble, pious idiot this time.* He put the figure down next to the dwarf and said firmly, 'We are both here.'

Joseph sat up straighter. 'We are both here, Jethro and Zephaniah, standing at the door of your catacombs, seeking entrance.'

Ruth's voice was icy, threatening.

'Naked you come into this place.
Naked you shall leave.

60

Between darkness and darkness, you shall find fear
and danger.
Turn back now,
before your hearts fail and your bodies betray you,
before you see horrors and do evil.'

Nick felt suddenly afraid—but that was ridiculous. It was only a game, for heaven's sake, and he'd played games like that dozens of times before.

But this was different from any game he'd played at the school club. There your mind was working on two levels all the time. One part of you was deep in the dungeons, wrestling with orcs or facing dragons, but you were still aware of ordinary things as well—how Benson rubbed his nose when he was working out combat points, or how long they'd got to play before the caretaker flung them out. Here, there was nothing to anchor him. Just the heavy-scented darkness, the tiny figures in the light—and Ruth's voice.

Joseph spoke from beside him. 'We shall not do evil because we do not come in our own strength alone. I charge you to let us go forward. By the power of the dog.'

Nick hadn't got a clue what that meant, but Ruth's voice hissed, sharp in the darkness, and his mouth went dry. Then she spoke.

'The door swings open, inwards. The catacombs are unlit.'

Joseph nudged Nick and hissed in his ear. 'You talk to her. I'll draw.' Carefully, he made the first marks on a new page in his book.

'OK,' muttered Nick. He raised his voice. 'We step inside and shine our torch around.'

Ruth continued in a steady voice. 'You are standing in a small cavern, low-roofed and rough-walled, about ten feet square. Ahead of you, a passage winds away into the darkness. From far down it, you can hear a distant scraping and scratching, but you see nothing.'

*Careful, now. Visualize it. Don't make any rash moves*, Nick thought. 'Can we see anything else?'

'On the left, there is a barred opening in the wall at

shoulder height. It shows nothing but darkness.'

'Does it open?'

'No.'

'And on the right?'

'The wooden door that has just opened to let you in.'

Joseph wriggled slightly, impatient to get on, but Nick still wasn't quite happy. There was something—

Then he got it. The door. It had to be that. He leaned sideways to mutter at Joseph.

'Should we look behind the door?'

In the torchlight, he saw Joseph's eyes widen as the message got through and he nodded agreement.

'We pull the door away from the wall,' Nick said loudly, 'so that we can see what is behind it.'

He saw Ruth's head go up, the fantastically-piled hair outlined against the strip of twilight. 'You dare?' she said tauntingly. 'Remember that you are Zephaniah. Zephaniah the coward and weakling. How do you find the courage to advise your companion to do this?'

Playing out of character. Damn it. She was right. And it was too late to get Joseph to be the one who suggested it. But there had to be a way of getting round that. There just *had* to.

And then he got it. He remembered what Joseph had said earlier on. *We do not come in our own strength alone.* That had to mean that there was someone or something backing them up. And Zephaniah might be a coward, but he had a thumping great score of fifteen for faith. Perhaps it wasn't so useless after all. Nick didn't know the rules about gods in the game, but he decided to take a chance.

'I trust in the one who protects me,' he said defiantly. 'I may be weak, but he is strong, and his strength gives me courage.'

As he said it, he felt a real creep, but it certainly did the trick. When Ruth answered, her voice was not so harsh. There was a note in it that was almost approval.

'Your faith is great and this makes a brave man of you, in spite of the shrinking of your flesh. You now have a bravery score of fifteen, and you can decide to move the door, if you wish.'

Wow. Some increase, Nick thought smugly. 'Right then. We move the door and shine our torch into the darkness behind it.'

'Bats!' Ruth spat the word. 'Dozens of vampire bats were hanging from a ledge behind the door. They fly up, to get away from the light, and escape through the grating.'

'Well done,' Joseph murmured. 'I wouldn't fancy having those following us down the passage.'

Nick grinned at him. 'We shine the torch round,' he said. 'To see if there is anything else behind the door.' There had to be some kind of reward for spotting the bats, surely.

He was right. 'Two slingshots made of stout cloth lie on a heap of pebbles,' Ruth said. 'And there is a jewelled dagger beside them, with an inscription carved into the handle.'

'We read the inscription.' Joseph was so eager that he got the words out before Nick could speak.

> *'I am most apt to skilled or unskilled hand.*
> *For I am DEATH whom no one can withstand.'*

Ruth's voice was neutral as she recited the rhyme, giving no clues, but Nick nearly laughed out loud. She didn't really think he was going to fall for that old trick, did she? *I am DEATH*—and nothing to say it wouldn't turn on its owner. That's the sort of weapon you need like a hole in the head.

'Don't touch it,' he hissed at Joseph.

'Think I'm daft?' Joseph grinned. 'I reckon we're safe with the slingshots, though. They're good biblical weapons.'

Biblical? Nick was lost for a second, until he remembered. David killed Goliath with a slingshot. This game certainly had some peculiar rules. 'We each take a slingshot,' he said, 'and put ten pebbles into our pockets. But we leave the dagger for some other idiot.'

'Very well.' Ruth was trying not to give anything away, but Nick could tell from her voice that they'd avoided one of her traps. 'Now are you ready to set out into the catacombs?'

Nick and Joseph looked at each other and grinned, their faces creasing into deep shadows in the torchlight. It was going to be all right, and they both knew it. They were adventurers together.

There was nothing like it, *nothing*, Nick thought triumphantly two hours later. He and Joseph didn't make a single mistake, in spite of the traps Ruth set. They dodged the demons who came out of a side passage, masquerading as lepers. They found their way through a submerged tunnel into a great carved cavern with flaming torches fixed to the walls, and they dodged a plague of giant, man-eating ants.

But the best moment of all was near the end. They were walking in the dark, to stop the ants following, and they were attacked by an unseen enemy. They both reacted like lightning, without needing to discuss it.

'The torch!'

It had to be that. If their enemy could see in the dark, the light *must* give them an advantage. Nick spelled it out. 'We light the torch and shine it, as quickly as we can, at the place the spear was thrown from.'

Got him! There was a wail from across the room. Not the Jezebel voice, but another, feeble and whining. 'The light! Turn out the light!'

'Let him come down so we can have a look at him,' Nick said. 'We'll cover his face to shut out the light once we've got him.'

'All right. You've got him,' Ruth said. Then the voice whined again. 'I'm the Nightwalker, good gentlemen. A poor, pale creature with no lids to my eyes. Have pity on me. Let me go back into the kind darkness.'

Nick looked across at Joseph. 'We can't just let him go, can we? What shall we do? Truss him up?'

Instantly, there was a shriek from across the room. 'Don't leave me here helpless! The ants will get me! The man-eating ants!'

Joseph's face went taut in the torchlight. 'He's right, you know. They're probably on their way here already. If we leave him helpless, he'll have had it.'

'Have mercy, lords,' screeched the Nightwalker. 'Let me go, and I'll be your faithful servant for ever.'

There was a moment's silence while Nick and Joseph stared at each other, weighing it up. Common sense and prudence on one side, and compassion on the other. In the school game, Nick wouldn't have hesitated a second. The

Nightwalker would have been trussed up at the side of the tunnel, probably with a knife in him, for good measure. But here, with Zephaniah . . .

Nick crossed his fingers hard. 'All right. We'll trust you. We let you go.'

Joseph nodded. 'I agree.'

Ruth's voice came evenly through the darkness. 'He is very small. As you let go of him, his fingers scrabble round, along the wall of the tunnel. A section of the wall slides away.' Her voice changed back to the Nightwalker's whine. 'This is the way, kind lords. Unless you take this hidden staircase, you'll never escape the ants.'

For a second, Nick closed his eyes. They'd done it. Against all the odds, they'd made the right decision. And they hadn't even needed to discuss it. They were thinking together. He grinned at Joseph in the torchlight. Before tonight, he'd had him marked down as a ditherer, a nice enough guy, but too meek-and-mild to be much use in an emergency. But now he felt the beginning of another feeling. Less scornful. More like respect.

Joseph must have felt something similar, because when Ruth finally disappeared into the wardrobe he muttered in Nick's ear. 'Got time for a coffee before you go back?'

'If you like.'

The kitchen was empty, and they sat one on each side of the table, rocking back in their chairs in the way that made Nick's mother go berserk. Joseph stared thoughtfully at Nick.

'You were right about it being better with two adventurers. It was great having someone else to discuss things with. And it had an effect on Ruth, too.'

'How do you mean?' Nick said.

'Oh, I don't know. Sharpened her up. Moved her out of the usual old groove. She knows what I'll take, and what makes me shudder, but with you—' He stopped and took a sip of his coffee.

'Go on.' Nick wasn't ready to leave it there. 'What's she going to do with me?'

Joseph took his time to answer. 'I think—you're an unknown area to her, you see. Not a Fisher. Not a girl. Not

65

one of the congregation. I think she'll be out to test you, to find what makes you crack.'

*. . . risking all trials,*
*and facing all knowledge . . .*

'Mental torture?' Nick said lightly.

'Thumbscrews of the soul.' Joseph stopped grinning. 'Don't laugh it off. It's not—I can't really explain. But Ruth's dead good at getting under your skin and she gets carried away sometimes.'

The darkness, the rustling skirts, the incense sticks— invisible Jezebel, whose voice came out of nowhere. Yes, that figured. There was something more than a game going on, something to do with real power and curiosity. But that was what made it all so intriguing. Nick nodded.

'Thanks for the warning.'

'That's all right. I have to take care of you, don't I? Seeing you're such a weakling.'

Suddenly they were grinning at each other again, and Nick was thinking how peculiar it was, having one conversation and making it stand in for something else. *It's great to be playing this game with you. I really like you. We're a good team.* That's what they really meant, both of them. But they could never have said it, not in a hundred years.

They looked round together as Ruth came down the stairs and opened the kitchen door. Her face was pale and shiny, as if she had just washed it ferociously, and her thick red hair was plaited into two tight braids. Shabby old brown skirt and jumper. Looking at her, Nick found it almost impossible to believe in Jezebel.

'Don't *I* get a cup of coffee?' she said sharply.

# Chapter 10

All the way back across the Marsh, in the dark, Nick sang. Marching songs, battle songs, ferocious football chants. They were going to do it, he and Joe. They were going to beat Jezebel hollow. They would fight their way through the catacombs, shoulder to shoulder, and when they found her lair, they would smash her! He was high on the game, exulting in their success and the fantastic, amazing way they got on together.

Which was probably why he lost his way.

He thought he knew the Marsh by now, that it was familiar ground. And that was why he let his attention wander. One moment he was on familiar ground, between a big barn and the farmhouse that always had its porch light on. Next time he looked, he was lost. Nothing but flat fields and ditches, with the odd hedge.

By the time he'd retraced his route and failed to find where he had gone wrong, he had lost all hope of seeing where he was going. It was completely dark, and he couldn't even see a light in the distance, across fields.

Only one thing for it. He'd just have to find a house somewhere and ask his way. If there had been even a single star visible he would have been happier. Then he could have told whether he was cycling round in circles. As it was, he just had to keep his fingers crossed.

It must have been another half an hour at least before he glanced up a left turn and saw a small cluster of houses at a crossroads. The place looked deserted, but there must be people behind those lighted windows. For a second he blew on his fingers, to warm them, and then he began to cycle up the road.

As he got closer, he could see that the nearest building had a telephone box beside it. Must be the local shop and post office. And there was a figure standing in the shadows outside it. He ought to be able to get some reliable directions there.

And then when he had almost reached the shop he heard the crash of breaking glass.

Afterwards, it amazed him that he had reacted so quickly. *Something wrong*, said his brain and, without working it out, he pulled into the side of the road. His bike lights went out as he stopped pedalling, and he laid the bike flat and slithered down the side of the ditch, grabbing hold of the top to keep himself just high enough to see what was going on.

The glass of the shop window had been broken from inside. He saw the figure on the pavement jump back as splinters sprayed outwards on to the pavement. Following them, almost while the glass was still spraying, a shape came bombing through the window, kicking a litter of tins and packets with it. At the same time, two more figures raced out of the shop door, throwing bottles that shattered into yet more fragments of glass. Nick caught the smell of bleach as well, squirted out of its plastic container like water from a water pistol.

It was all so quick that he barely had time to catch his breath. One moment he had been cycling along in silence, not hearing a thing—they must have been moving as quietly as cats inside the shop. The next moment there had been this explosion of wrecking and disaster.

Then the figures were leaping on to the bikes they had left outside the shop. The engines spat and accelerated suddenly towards Nick, and he crouched low in his ditch, hiding his face so that it wouldn't show white in the beam of the headlamps.

As soon as the bikes were past, he looked up, at the backs of the riders. They were already twenty or thirty yards away, but even at that distance he knew who they were. Especially the last rider. Nick knew the hunch of the shoulders and the way the collar of the jacket was turned half up and half down. And he had never seen another bike like Terry's ancient Yamaha, anywhere in the area.

*They're stupid. It's so early. They'll never get away.* Already people were yelling and car engines were starting up. Nick crouched in his ditch, hardly able to breathe, waiting for disaster.

Instead, as the cars swept down the road after them, the bikes accelerated suddenly. At the same time, their lights went out, all together. It sounded as if they were set for a long chase, but the acceleration was only for a moment. Immediately afterwards, the sound of the engines changed, growing rougher and slower, and Nick panicked. They must be crazy. If they travelled at that speed, the cars were sure to catch up.

But instead of chasing after the bikes, the cars slowed down and stopped, just at the point where the headlamps had gone out. The drivers got out to talk to each other, banging their doors, and a voice swore sharply through the darkness.

Listening to the sound of the engines fading in the distance, curiously spread out, as though they were fanning apart, Nick suddenly realized what had happened. The bikers had left the road. They must have jumped the drainage ditch, going straight ahead at a bend, and taken off across the fields where the cars couldn't follow. Because their headlamps were out, the watchers couldn't even see where they were making for, to cut them off.

It must all have been worked out in advance. The place must have been reconnoitred and every rider must have known where to leave the road. At least one of the bikers was very, very cunning.

Nick was so relieved that he felt feeble. At least they'd escaped this time. No one could have had a chance to take a number or recognize any of the riders.

Except him.

He had plenty of time to think that over. Stuck in the ditch, freezing cold, and awkwardly scrabbling at the side he had to wait another half an hour or so before the cars gave up and went home. Then, finally, he crawled out and got back on his bicycle.

It was a long ride home, in the cold and the wet. He had to fight the wind all the way to Holney, and by the time he got home he hardly had the energy to put his bike away. He staggered through the kitchen door, grabbed a handful of chocolate biscuits, and made straight for his room.

As he went past the lounge, he could hear the television blaring away and his father's raised voice speaking above the noise—'What rubbish!'—'The idiots!' He went by the door carefully, on tiptoe. The last thing he wanted was to get lumbered with talking to his mum and dad.

Upstairs everything was dark and quiet. No sign of Terry. Nick went into his bedroom as fast as he could, not letting himself wonder where Terry was, or what he was doing. He had to forget all that. Forget what he had seen and what it meant.

It had nothing to do with him.

All he wanted was peace and quiet. No one bothering him or asking him questions.

But he had only just sat down on his bed when he heard feet on the stairs. A second later, there was a tap on the door.

'Nick?'

It was his mother's voice, soft and a bit nervous. No prizes for guessing why she was the one who had come up. Dad had sent her. Nick could hear the words in his mind. *He's very late. Someone ought to say something to him.* That's all it would have taken. His mother would have been on her feet at once.

'Yeah?' he said, taking a deep breath.

Mrs Miller pushed the door open and peeped round. 'So you are home. I thought I heard you.'

Nick nodded.

'Are you all right?'

'Of course I'm all right. I—' But his tongue froze. All he could think was *I mustn't tell her. I mustn't let her know what I saw.*

His mother hovered in the doorway and he wanted to yell at her to make up her mind. *Either come in or go out.* But that would be fatal. At the first yell, his dad would be up, doing the don't-you-speak-to-your-mother-like-that bit. Nick managed a smile.

'Do you want me for something?'

'No.' She said it uncertainly and then repeated it. 'No, it's just that you didn't look in and tell me you were back. I do like to know that you're safe.'

'But why shouldn't I be safe?'

'No—no reason.' She glanced away to avoid his eyes and he saw her look hard at his hands, which were still holding the chocolate biscuits.

Nick looked down at them himself. They were trembling, actually shaking, as if he was an old man. He put them behind his back, with a mental groan. That was it. Now, surely, Mum would insist on knowing what he had been doing. He swallowed and concentrated hard. *I mustn't tell her. I mustn't let her get it out of me.*

But what she said was, 'If you're hungry, I can easily cook you something. How about a pizza?'

For a second he couldn't believe his ears. A pizza? Did she think he was trembling because he wanted a *pizza?* Suddenly, perversely, he was furious with her.

'No thanks,' he lied. 'I couldn't eat a thing. I had tea with the Fishers, remember?'

He heard his voice shake as he said it, and he knew that his control over it was fragile. He was weak with shock and anger, cold and confusion, and a small, treacherous part of his mind wanted her to treat him like a small child. He wanted her to force the truth out of him and then take care of the whole difficult problem.

But she didn't even look straight at him. Standing in the doorway, running her finger up and down the frame, she said, 'You're very late back.'

He could see that even that was an effort to say. 'I got lost!' he snapped.

'Oh dear,' Mrs Miller said. But all at once she sounded different. Relieved. 'I just thought—well I thought something might have happened to you.'

*Worried were you, mother dear? Did you think I might have met up with a nasty rough gang of bikers out on the Marsh? Why don't you say so, then? Why do you keep dancing round and round the subject? You can see I'm shaking all over.* Another prod, another little annoyance, and Nick would have shouted it all at her, not caring what happened next.

Suddenly, irrelevantly, he remembered the fuss Joseph had made when Thomas wanted one of Ruth's toffees. All that talk of stealing. Well, there was nothing like that in the

Miller family. You could rob a bank, beat up six old ladies, sit shaking with terror in your bedroom—and all anyone would say was *Are you all right, dear?*

Didn't she know something was going on? Didn't she care?

'I'm OK,' he said gruffly.

'And you don't want anything to eat? Certain?'

Nick shook his head.

His mother smiled suddenly as if she had completed a difficult duty. 'Well, I'll say goodnight, then. Don't be too late in bed.'

'No. Goodnight.'

And that was it. End of a meaningless, nothing conversation.

It was only as Mrs Miller went downstairs that Nick realized the conversation had had one use. It had saved him from thinking. Now there was nothing in between him and the sound of the bikes in his head.

# Chapter 11

For three days he sweated it out on his own. Terry was invisible—always in bed or out of the house—and Nick was grateful for that. He didn't know what he would say to him if they met. But there was no one else he could talk to. He walked about as if he had been knocked silly, with thoughts buzzing restlessly in his head. Round and round and round.

Everything had been simple up till then. He was in a game with Joseph and Ruth and when he was playing, he could sit back and enjoy it. But all the time, at the back of his mind, he knew that he had another reason for being with them, a secret, exciting reason, a bit like being a double agent.

Just another game.

Only that had all changed, now he'd seen the bikes. He couldn't go on fooling himself. Couldn't pretend that he didn't know what The Company did on those long rides in the dark, or hope it had nothing to do with him. What they did was dangerous and serious, and he was in it up to the neck. He didn't know what that meant, or what he ought to do, but it was all he could think about.

Then, on Saturday, he got home at lunchtime, after a disastrous football match. He hadn't been able to concentrate for more than two minutes together and Knocker Bradley had sworn steadily at him, all through the second half.

That was when Terry called him. Nick heard his voice as he reached the top of the stairs.

'That you? Here a minute.'

Nick stopped and looked at the half-open door of Terry's bedroom. 'I've got things to do.'

'Won't take long.'

Nick hesitated a second longer, then walked across the landing and pushed the door open.

They were all there. Terry and Leo were sitting on the bed, eating chips out of the paper, Bill was on the floor by

73

the record player, and Donna was pacing round the room.

'Come in.' Leo waved a hand. 'Plenty of room on the floor.'

They were all looking up now. Nick wished he could turn round and go away, but he knew that wouldn't do. He slid inside, stepping carefully round a pile of records, and shut the door behind him. 'What's up?'

'Has something got to be up?' Terry glanced round at the others, innocently. 'Do you get the feeling my baby brother doesn't appreciate my company?'

'Perhaps he's got other things on his mind,' Bill said drily.

'Perhaps he has. Been out on the Marsh a lot, have you, Nick?' Terry lay back on the bed, with his hands behind his head. *Relaxing*, Nick thought. Then he corrected himself. There was nothing relaxed about Terry. Even from the other side of the room, Nick could feel the tension that filled his whole body.

'Yes,' he said warily. 'I've been out there a few times.'

'You must really be at home there by now.' Leo picked the last chip out of the paper. 'One of the family, are you?'

At home. One of the family. They didn't seem quite the right words to describe how he felt in that bleak house behind the shop. Nick shrugged. 'I get on pretty well with Fisher and his sister.'

'You do?' Leo raised one agile eyebrow. 'Bosom friends, are you? Blood brothers?'

Nick shrugged again, and Donna whirled round suddenly from the window, glaring so fiercely that he stepped backwards until he bumped against the door.

'I don't know why you're all pussy-footing about. It's obvious what's happened. The kid's got thick with Holy Joe, and he's ratted on us.'

'Donna, don't get so worked up,' said Bill. He reached up a hand and pulled her down to sit beside him on the floor. 'What business is it of ours? Nick can make friends with whoever he likes, can't he?'

His voice was very quiet and slow, and ten times more threatening than Donna's had been. Nick stared back defiantly.

'That's right. Joe Fisher's my friend. You're just Terry's mates.'

'*Just* Terry's mates!' Leo chuckled. 'That puts us in our places, doesn't it? What are you going to do about that, Bill?'

They all looked round at Bill, waiting, and for the first time Nick realized who was the leader of the group. Bill smiled placidly.

'It's nothing to do with any of us, is it? Let the kid go. He's got his own life to lead.'

Nick watched him carefully, puzzled, expecting something else, but Bill just waved a hand.

'Go on. If you've got things to do, just go and get on with them. We don't want to interfere with you, do we?'

The others didn't know what was going on either. Donna moved, as if she wanted to get up, but Bill grabbed her shoulder and kept her where she was. Nick decided that he had better go while he had the chance. Fumbling behind him for the door handle, he turned it quickly.

He had the door half open, when Bill spoke again. Very softly. Almost as if he were thinking aloud.

'Of course, we hope you'll remember who—introduced you to Joseph Fisher. Who gave you the chance to go to his house the first time. I'm sure you'll be properly grateful for that.'

Nick froze, holding his breath. No need to ask what Bill meant by *properly grateful*.

'Well?' The voice was still quiet, but this time it was very sharp.

'Suppose—' Nick took a deep breath and forced himself to get the words out. 'Suppose I'm not. There's nothing you can do about it.'

'You sneaky little—' Donna was half on her feet this time, but Bill pulled her down again.

'Stop it, Don. Nick's right. What can we do?' Bill was almost purring. 'We'll just have to put up with it if he's ungrateful. And of course we'll have to—'

He paused, and Nick gripped the door handle harder. This was it. 'You'll have to what?'

Bill smiled benignly at him. 'We'll have to warn the

Fishers about what kind of person you are. Just so you don't upset *them* as well.'

Leo's sudden shout of laughter broke into the tense silence, but it was no kind of relief. Nick felt the door handle growing damp and slippery in his hand and when he looked across at Terry, his brother's eyes slid away.

'Nothing dramatic, of course,' Bill said, thoughtfully. 'Just a little note. Something like—*Are you sure it's wise to let Nick Miller know where your safe is?*'

Nick closed his eyes and swallowed hard. 'They wouldn't take any notice. They're not the sort of people who'd listen to anonymous letters.'

Suddenly Bill's smile was very wide. 'Of course they wouldn't! I'm sure they'd ask you about it, and take your word. Whatever you said.'

He was right. Nick could just imagine the scene. The whole Fisher family would greet him next time he got there. Mr Fisher would tell him about the letter, with Mrs Fisher at his side, looking grieved and waiting to have it denied. Joseph would be solemn and Ruth would be sharp but fair—and they'd all make such a *thing* out of it. Nick knew that he would never be able to face them all and brazen it out. Either he would confess, or he would run away.

And that meant there was no choice for him. He didn't have to decide if he would side with the Fishers or The Company. If he ratted on The Company and jacked in the quest, then that was the end of his friendship with Joseph as well. It was so neat that it took his breath away.

But he wasn't just knuckling under meekly. He took a deep breath and launched out. 'Don't you think you ought to level with me? You set me up. You've dropped me in this without giving me a chance to choose. Don't I get to know what it's all about?'

At first he didn't think he was going to get an answer. The others looked at Bill and Bill just smiled. But suddenly Terry marched across the room, pushed Nick out of the way, and threw the door open.

'What can you hear?' he said sharply. 'Go on. Listen.'

Nick listened, but all he could make out was his father's voice, rumbling away downstairs. 'It's just Mum and Dad talking.'

'Talking!' Terry laughed without sounding amused. 'They're not *talking*. Dad's boring Mum with his next great plan after the barbecue. Heard about it?'

Nick shook his head. He couldn't see what that had to do with the quest.

Terry laughed again. 'He's going to have an all-night video party. Hire another video—so he can show two different films at once—and have a barrel of beer in the kitchen. Pathetic, isn't it?'

'I don't see why,' Nick said. 'Why shouldn't he have parties like that, if he enjoys them?'

'But he doesn't, does he?' said Terry. 'He hates barbecue food—and he was so busy cooking at the barbecue that he never talked to any of the people he'd invited. And it'll be the same with this. He's just showing off, proving that he can do things on a bigger scale than the neighbours. He's too *dead* to enjoy anything properly.'

'Brain dead,' murmured Leo. 'Just like my parents.'

Nick shrugged. 'So what's that got to do with what you lot are up to?'

'I want to know I'm alive,' Donna said fiercely. 'I can't stand *boredom*. You know where you are when you're in danger, because it's real. And when you're going out to face it with your friends—'

The Company. Nick was suddenly so envious that he couldn't speak.

'That's when you get really close to people,' Bill said softly. 'When you face danger together, with no one to pick you up and kiss it better if things go wrong.'

Nick closed his eyes for a second. It was like having his dreams step out into real life. 'So where does that leave me?'

'That's it, isn't it?' Terry said. 'You can choose. Be part of it—one of us—or be like them.' He waved a hand contemptuously towards the sound of their father's voice.

Bill nodded, but his face had sharpened. 'Only you haven't got for ever to decide. We want to know.'

'We want to know *now*,' Donna said.

Somewhere at the back of his head, Nick knew he ought to tell them he wasn't going to spy for them any more. He ought to screw up Terry's letter about the quest and chuck it back at them all, even if that meant he had to pay Terry ten pounds. That's what Joseph would have done.

But Joseph hadn't spent years and years dreaming about The Company. Longing to be part of it.

'What's the matter?' said Terry. 'Is the quest too difficult for you? Or are you just scared?'

Something about the way he said *scared* made Nick cringe inside and he almost shouted the words that came automatically on to his tongue.

'It's nothing to do with being scared. I've discovered half those things already. I can find out the rest of them whenever I want.'

There was a long, still silence. Then Bill spoke, very quietly.

'OK. You've got a week.'

And that was it. Dismissed. Leo got up to put on another record and Donna lay back and closed her eyes while Bill pulled a strand of her hair gently through his fingers.

Nick stared at them all for a moment, then stalked out and marched along the landing to his own bedroom. But as he shut himself in, he was ice-cold.

*A week.* He must be mad. Now he'd agreed they were liable to hold him to it, and most of what he had found out so far was sheer luck.

He pulled the crumpled bit of paper out of his blazer pocket and stared down at the list.

1. *How does the burglar alarm in the shop work? (and where are the keys kept?)*

He knew how the burglar alarm worked, more or less, thanks to Thomas, but he hadn't got a clue where to find the keys.

2. *Where is the money put when the shop's shut?*

In a safe? Under the bed? Inside Susie's pillow? What chance did he have of finding *that* out, for heaven's sake?

3. *When does it go to the bank?*

OK, so Joseph had told him that by mistake. Bank day was on Wednesday, when the shop closed early and Mr and Mrs

Fisher went to the cash and carry. Visit Gran on Tuesday, bank day on Wednesday, and Jezebel on Monday and Wednesday evenings. It was simple to find out what the Fishers did every day, because they had such boring lives. But finding where they kept their money was a different matter.

And anyway Joseph wasn't a stranger any more.

Nick looked down at his hands. They were clenched hard into fists, screwing up the piece of paper. He had to decide between losing everything—his friends and the game and ten pounds and his chance to join The Company—and helping to rob the shop. And he knew the Fishers well enough by now to have some idea of what that robbery would mean to them.

It was the kind of choice you got in a game, but in a game there'd be an answer. You could work out what risks you took if you made the wrong decision, or what your companions might face if you abandoned them. But how could he weigh up the two sides of *this* choice?

Nick pulled the Star Warrior out of his pocket and stood him in his place on the chest of drawers. What would he choose?

It took him a long time to realize that he didn't know how to make that sort of decision. He didn't even know how to begin thinking about it. He would just have to wait and see what he did.

# Chapter 12

Forget about it. That was what he ought to do. And he thought he'd found a foolproof way of shutting it out of his mind. All he had to do was plant himself in front of the television, to watch the sport with Dad.

That worked all right for the rest of Saturday. Mr Miller liked someone around while he was watching. Someone to dig in the ribs and shout at.

'Did you *see* that? The ref must be crazy. Look at the replay, Nick. That was a penalty if ever I saw one.'

On and on, without even giving the other person time to reply.

'—now that's a brilliant shot. That *is* a brilliant shot. I haven't seen a goal like that since—'

It was good value. Just what Nick wanted. If his thoughts wandered for a second, his father would be shaking him by the shoulder.

'Stop daydreaming, boy. You're missing the action.'

But on Sunday the television broke down. Mr Miller went off to sulk until the repair man appeared—he hated any of his gadgets going wrong—and Nick was left to his own thoughts.

Now there was no escaping from the choice. Who was he going to side with? The Company or the Fishers? Terry or Joseph? It rattled round and round his head and, by Monday morning, he knew that he had to discuss it with someone.

For a minute or two, as he was cycling to school, he thought he might try explaining it all to Livingstone. He wasn't daft—he'd understand. And if he could get him on his own, without Parker, Livingstone would keep it all a secret.

But that idea vanished as soon as he walked into the cloakroom to hang up his jacket. There was a crowd of people in the boys' cloakroom, heads bent together. As Nick passed, the crowd parted and Livingstone stuck his head out of the middle.

'Here, Miller, how about this one? Ever seen anything like it?'

Livingstone had a legendary collection of dirty pictures. Usually they were good for a giggle, but just then Nick couldn't even be bothered to think about them. He pretended to glance at the photograph and tried to push past. But that didn't fool Livingstone, of course.

'What's up, Miller? Frightened your friend *Saint* Joseph Fisher is going to come by and catch you looking at something naughty?'

There was a roar of laughter from the others.

'Yeah. Smack, smack, Miller.'

'They'd never let you in the Christian Union then!'

'Better go and have a cold shower!'

But Livingstone wasn't laughing. He stared hard at Nick, with the pictures held out towards him, and suddenly Nick realized that he was asking a real question. *OK, Miller, whose side are you on? Fisher's or mine?*

For a second, Nick wondered what Joseph would have said about the pictures. He couldn't imagine Joseph—. Then he ducked the question.

'Oh come *on*, Livingstone. Yawn, yawn. Pictures like that are kids' stuff. When are you going to grow up a bit?'

It should have worked. With Livingstone it was always best to attack. The harder you hit him, the more he believed what you said, because that was how things were in the Livingstone family.

But there were other kids around today. Livingstone wasn't just going to knuckle under and lose face. He stared at Nick for another second and then called over his shoulder.

'Hey, Parker, I think we'll have to look for someone else to join in our poker game today. Miller's busy *growing up*.'

It was a test. You didn't get into Livingstone's poker game unless he trusted you, because the Head went mad if people were caught gambling. And if you got cut out of poker, it had a way of spreading. Nick felt a space open round him as some of the other boys stepped back.

He might have things to think about, but he wasn't ready to be on his own all the time. He managed a loud, jeering laugh.

'What's the matter, Livingstone? Can't you afford to play with me any more? You still owe me a pound from last week remember.'

For an instant the whole thing hung in the balance. The boys who were turning away waited to see if there was going to be a fight, and Parker took a step away from Livingstone, to show that he wasn't in it if there was.

Then Livingstone held out his bundle of pictures. 'Yeah, well, I haven't got a pound, have I? Want to borrow my pictures for a bit instead?'

Nick looked down at the pictures. No one had ever been allowed to borrow them before. And it didn't take a genius to guess what would happen if he turned the offer down. Livingstone was watching him hard, and it was still the same question really. *Fisher or me?*

Nick took the pictures with a grin and put them in his pocket. 'Just this once then,' he said. 'But if I win at lunchtime, I'm having real money.'

Livingstone grinned back at him and the tension in the cloakroom suddenly vanished as though something had been settled. Boys started to shuffle off to registration and Livingstone and Parker waited while Nick hung up his bag.

But nothing was really settled, not inside Nick's head. He had fended off the questions, but all he had found out was that he couldn't let Livingstone in on his problem. There was only one person who would understand what was bugging him.

Joseph.

Nick missed out on his school lunch at twelve fifteen and went to track Joseph down. He was sitting in the warm sheltered corner round at the back of the boiler house, eating his sandwiches and staring up at the dismal grey sky.

'Hi.' Nick sat down on the step beside him.

'Hallo.' It wasn't quite a question, but Joseph sounded surprised.

'I've been thinking about the game.' *Careful, now. Take it slowly.* There was no way he could explain it directly. Not to Joseph.

Joseph glanced round, but there was no one in sight and he relaxed. 'Something worrying you? I thought it was good on Wednesday.'

'It was great. But—' Nick hesitated a moment, trying to make sure he had chosen the best way of coming at what he wanted, because if he blew it he'd have ruined everything. 'Especially that last bit, with the Nightwalker. Ruth thought she had us fooled there, didn't she?'

'I think she was pretty surprised you got it right.' Joseph grinned. 'She was ready to jump on you for playing out of character, you know, if you'd left him to be eaten by the ants.'

'Virtuous old Zephaniah, you mean?' Nick tried to sound casual. 'So what would have happened if I had played him out of character?'

Joseph shrugged. 'Terrible fever? Poisonous gases in the air affecting your judgement? She'd have produced some explanation like that. You would have suffered, believe me.'

'Dead cunning.' Nick stared out across the football field for a moment, almost holding his breath. Because now he was going to ask the real question. 'So it's like real life, is it? You do the thing that is best for you, that you can get something out of. All that about trusting the Nightwalker because it was the right thing to do was just a load of hot air?'

Joseph chewed on his sandwich for a while before he answered. Then he said, 'How could we have guessed it would help us? No, we had a straight choice between bashing him or being merciful. And he said he was sorry, so we had to believe him.'

There seemed to be a heavy weight on Nick's chest, interfering with his breathing. 'Why?'

'Because—because the world can't function unless you give people the benefit of the doubt.' Joseph sounded as though it was all dead simple. 'Even people like the Nightwalker can choose to be good.'

'You think they would, in real life?' Nick said. 'You think everyone worries about *good* and *bad*?'

It was really hard to breathe now. Surely Joseph would guess what he was really asking. *What does goodness matter? Why should I think twice about helping Terry's gang to do your shop over, if it's best for me?* But all Joseph did was hold out a sandwich.

'Want one?'

Nick took it automatically and bit into it to avoid having to talk any more. It was filled with peanut butter, spread thin, and as soon as he'd taken the first mouthful he realized that it was Joseph's last one. All he could do was chew it slowly, as if it was being appreciated, even though it tasted like wood chips.

'Who cares what everyone worries about?' Joseph said at last. 'I thought we were talking about what's right, not about what people think.'

*What's right.* He said it as if he was talking about something real, like an iron bar or a stone wall, and suddenly Nick felt unreasonably angry.

'So you think I ought to take all your piddling little rules on board, do you? Just because they're *right*?'

Joseph looked down at his feet. 'They're not "piddling little rules". They're a system, like a map, to help you find your way through things.'

'Great. And who's going to show it to me? A holy angel in a flash of lightning?'

Joseph's fists were clenched and he was still looking down, but his voice came out quiet and strong. 'It's not that simple, you know. I think—' He swallowed a couple of times. '—I think it's up to us. We've got to make sense of it for ourselves. Make our own maps.'

*Make our own maps.* But that was no help. No help at all. Nick could see the game maps in front of them, as plain as if they were lying on the ground. Joseph's neat little black lines, clear and sharp and sure of themselves. And his own, that he'd made for Benson's game—jumbled scribbles with the wrong measurements and the writing all tangled together.

'Rubbish!' he said angrily. 'You wouldn't talk like that if you'd ever had any real problems to cope with. There isn't anywhere like you're jabbering about. No neat little country with tidy, fixed paths and clear boundaries. Life— *real* life—is chaos and what you're making is just a map of nowhere!'

Pow! Got him! Joseph was annoyed, even a bit hurt. Another minute, thought Nick, and his cool would break.

He'd be yelling too, perhaps even hitting out, and that would prove . . .

What would it prove? That Joseph wasn't perfect? So why was that so important? Before he could work it out, there was a sudden loud whoop from the corner of the boiler house. Parker's voice.

'There you are, Miller. Thought you were coming to play p—er—hrrrm.'

The way the word was cut off was an insult to Joseph, and Parker meant it to be. He had the usual jeering grin on his silly fat face. Livingstone, coming round the corner a step behind, was watching hard to see what was going on.

It was odd how they always turned up when he was talking to Joseph. Almost as though they were spying on him. Almost as if they knew . . .

All of a sudden, as they prowled towards him, Nick turned cold. No one would trust Parker with a real secret— but Livingstone was Donna's brother. Suppose he was part of the set-up?

As clearly as if he had seen it happen, he imagined Livingstone standing in the changing room, with Joseph's wallet in his hand. Glancing round with a weasel-sharp face. Then, when no one was watching, opening the zip and slipping the wallet into his bag.

Livingstone, his friend.

Nick closed his eyes for a second. He didn't need any proof. He was absolutely certain it had started like that. The Company had got hold of Joseph's wallet and seen the figure of the dwarf, and someone—Terry?—had said *We could put Nick in there. Set him up to make friends with Fisher.*

The scene played itself in his head. All The Company laughing, and Donna adding her little bit. *My brother can plant the wallet. He'll think that's a great joke.*

Livingstone's voice broke into his thoughts. 'What's up with you then, Miller? Aren't you going to say goodbye to your little friend?'

Opening his eyes, Nick saw that Joseph had grabbed his things and made off. Already, his hand was on the handle of the gym door. Nick yelled after him.

'Hey, Fisher! See you tonight, at your place. OK?'

Joseph hesitated for a second. Then he turned and grinned. 'OK. See you then.'

As he vanished into the gym lobby, Nick turned back to the others, defiantly. Parker gave a loud, jeering yodel, but Livingstone just nodded, once. He knew what was going on all right. Nick felt weak when he remembered that he had nearly confided in him. That would have given the game away. He was ready to bet that anything he said would have gone straight back to Donna.

For a second he felt horribly lonely. Then he made himself snap out of it. At least he would be playing Jezebel again after school. That was something to look forward to. He managed to look quite cheerful as he went off to play poker.

# Chapter 13

It felt as though the end of the day would never come. The poker game went on and on, boringly—even though he won another fifty pence—and afternoon school was even worse. As Nick blundered his way through French and social studies, every minute seemed like an hour.

He wished he could take off for the Fishers' straight from school, but he hadn't been asked. He had to go home and eat the meal Mum had cooked for him, and that was a hurdle as well, because she was fretting about how dangerous it was on the Marsh.

As she served out his tea, especially early, she had a go at him. 'That gang's getting really rough. Much worse. They broke into two more shops last week and smashed them up. And it's always out on the Marsh.'

'*Mum.*' Nick took the plate of steak and chips and sat down at the breakfast bar. 'I'm not a shop.'

'No, but—why can't your friends come here for a change?'

Nick tried to imagine Ruth crouched in his neat, new wardrobe, or burning her incense sticks on his chest of drawers. His father would be sniffing outside the door within ten minutes, trying to work out what they were smoking.

'It's all right, Mum. Honest.' He began to chop up his dinner, all together, so that he could eat it fast and get away. 'The gang won't hurt *me.*'

He'd said it without thinking, not meaning anything in particular. But as he jammed the first forkful of food into his mouth, he looked up at his mother and saw that she had gone white. What had he said?

*The gang won't hurt me.*

But why had that terrified her?

As soon as she realized he was watching her, she turned away and clattered around, doing things for everyone else's meal. Suddenly Nick understood. She suspected about the

87

gang and she had been afraid that he was going to tell her. She was desperate not to know.

That was how his parents always were. They didn't want anything to disturb the bright, shiny image they'd made. The perfect family in the perfect house.

All at once the steak in his mouth seemed tough and tasteless and he had to force it down, gulping it before he had chewed it properly.

Suppose he said, *Mum, I'm in trouble. I don't know whether to help Terry and his mates rob a shop or not.* What would she do? Would she help him, or would she just cry. Or—worst of all—would she just pretend she hadn't heard?

He didn't dare try it. Instead, he finished his meal as fast as he could, called 'Goodbye!' and went out to get his bike, without giving his mother another chance to argue. If only he could get away to the Fishers' and play Jezebel, at least things would be straightforward for an hour or two.

But even the road seemed to be against him. Every single traffic light was red. Lorries backed out and blocked the road, old ladies stepped off the pavement in front of him, and slow tractors with heavy loads waited until he was almost there before they pulled out. After half an hour of it, he was fuming.

When he got through Holney Fen, he thought he was safe at last. It was getting too dark for farm vehicles and he hadn't ever seen much else on those roads. Time to go full speed and make up for all the delays.

That was why he didn't notice the glass. Not until it crunched under his front wheel and he felt the sudden irregular thud of a flat tyre. Then he peered down and saw the remains of the broken bottle that some kind and thoughtful person had smashed, slowly, over ten yards.

Even if he had been carrying a puncture kit, there wouldn't have been a chance of doing anything. It was coming up to half-past six, with black clouds chopping off any remaining light, and he was a couple of miles out from Holney Fen, and three or four miles from Holney Seas End. All he could do was decide which way to start pushing. He swore quietly, under his breath, and then again, not so quietly, because there was something very satisfying about bellowing his rage over the dark flat fields. Then he began the long trudge towards Holney Seas End, still muttering.

He had been walking for about ten minutes when a car came up behind him and hooted gently. He stopped in mid-word, turned round and gave it two fingers, just to show that he wasn't going to be pushed around. The driver hooted again and called through the window.

'Nick.'

Confusion. Embarrassment. How was he supposed to guess that it was Ruth in the car? He hadn't even known that she could drive.

'What's up?' she called. 'Something wrong with your bike?'

Nick shielded his eyes against the glare of the headlamps. 'Yeah. Puncture. Broken bottle on the road.'

'Oh yes, I saw that. I stopped and cleared it away, because I thought someone might go through it without noticing.'

*OK, OK, Saint Ruth. I get the message.* That hadn't even occurred to Nick. But Ruth didn't go on about it. She jumped out and opened the back of the estate car.

'You can shove your bike in here. I've done all the deliveries, so there's plenty of room. And I expect Joe'll do your puncture for you. He's the Puncture King.'

That figured, given his geriatric bike. Nick turned and started wheeling his own bike back towards Ruth. 'Thanks. I really thought I'd have to walk the whole way.'

Ruth did not smile. 'Put the bike in carefully,' she said, 'so you don't bump the dog or squash the tomatoes. I'll tie the rope round it.'

She made the knot quickly and deftly, and they both climbed into the car. As she started up the engine again, she looked sideways at Nick. 'You were lucky I came along. You could wait for hours on this bit of road without seeing a soul.'

'Shudder,' said Nick. 'It's pretty wild and lonely out here, isn't it? But I suppose that's what you like.'

Ruth slowed down and changed gear bumpily at a corner. 'Me?'

'Yes. I mean—' He stopped, not sure what to say, but remembering how she strode over the saltings with the dog. 'You always seem to be the one who enjoys living out here.'

'I hate it.'

Pow. No explanations. Just a bald statement in her usual flat voice. Nick nearly fell off his seat. 'But you're always out there—walking the dog—and I—'

Ruth jammed on the brakes and turned the last corner. 'You can walk anywhere,' she said shortly. 'But that's all there is here. No jobs, nothing to do, no one under thirty to talk to. And the shop.'

It was in sight now and she glared at it suddenly, as if her eyes were flame-throwers.

'You hate that as well,' Nick said slowly. 'Don't you?'

He thought Ruth wasn't going to answer. She pulled up at the double gates that led into the back yard, and jumped down to open them before Nick even realized where they were. But when she climbed back into the car, she sat still for a moment, staring at the back of the shop.

'Being here is tearing our family to bits,' she said, as if she were talking to herself, as if Nick weren't there at all. 'If only we could *go*, it might be all right, but—'

'The crack in the foundations,' Nick murmured, before he could stop himself.

The minute the words were out, he knew it was a mistake to have said them. Ruth scowled and shoved the gear lever forward, revving the engine noisily. Nick said the first thing that came into his head, to try and put her in a better temper.

'You know what you ought to do, don't you? Widen that crack of yours and drop a bomb down it. Your insurance probably covers you against explosions.' Now he came to think of it, that was rather a clever idea. 'Hey yes, how about that? Reckon you could get away with it?'

It was only a joke, of course. The idea of a good little Fisher like Ruth plotting to cheat the insurance company was only good for a giggle. But she didn't show any signs of giggling. In fact, Nick didn't think she had heard at all. She backed the car into its place and turned off the engine without a word or a smile.

'Want me to bring you in some plastic explosive next time I come?' he said cheerfully.

And suddenly she turned on him. Swivelled round in her seat and glared with black, fierce eyes.

'That's just the sort of thing you *would* think of, isn't it? Someone like you always has an easy way out.'

It knocked the breath out of Nick. Not what she said— he didn't need to be psychic to know that Ruth had a pretty bad opinion of him—but the look in her eyes. He almost saw flames shooting out of them. She had planned that explosion, or something like it, a million times in the privacy of her own head. Nick had a sudden picture of the paraffin store at the side of the shop, sharp and clear as if it had been transferred directly from her brain to his.

'So why not?' he said softly. 'Why not?' and this time he was serious.

Ruth turned away and opened her door. 'It would be stealing from the insurance company,' she said shortly. Then she went.

The dog leaped over the seat to follow her and by the time Nick had got his breath back and caught her up, Ruth was halfway to the kitchen door. Locked into her usual chilly stiffness.

'I expect Joseph will still be putting the little ones to bed,' she muttered. 'We're late today. You'd better come into the kitchen and have a cup of coffee.'

'Thanks,' Nick said, following her through the kitchen door.

His first thought as he stepped inside was, *Well, there's one little one at least who's not being put to bed*. Thomas was standing beside the kitchen table, with his bottom lip stuck out stubbornly, and his parents one on each side of him. Heaped up on the table was a collection of small polythene bags full of coins and notes.

'I didn't,' Thomas said stubbornly. 'I didn't take them.'

Ruth looked sharply from Thomas to the pile of money. 'What's happened?'

'The keys have disappeared,' said Mrs Fisher. She looked very tired.

'I've told you a million times, it's stupid to keep them in

91

that drawer.' Ruth gave a loud, exasperated sigh.

'They can't be far,' Mrs Fisher said wearily. 'I locked the front door of the shop at closing time—I must have done, because I always do it. And I put the keys away in the proper place. I'm certain.'

She patted the wooden drawer in the side of the kitchen table as she spoke, and somewhere at the back of Nick's mind something went click. He couldn't have said if he was still doing the quest, but the information registered automatically. *Keys in the kitchen-table drawer.*

Ruth grabbed Thomas by the shoulder. 'Come on, Thomas, stop fooling about. You must have had the keys.'

Thomas's bottom lip trembled and he bit at the top one, forcing himself not to cry. He was a tough little kid, thought Nick, but he was lying. He'd had those keys all right, you could tell from his eyes. Why didn't they belt it out of him?

But that wasn't the Fishers' style, of course. Mr Fisher looked at Ruth. 'Leave it to me,' he said quietly.

He sat down and pulled Thomas gently to stand in front of him. Mrs Fisher and Ruth watched over his shoulders, so that Thomas was confronting three serious faces.

'Now then, Thomas,' Mr Fisher said gently, 'you know the keys are important, don't you?'

Thomas nodded. Nick guessed that he didn't dare speak in case he cried.

Mr Fisher held his hand. 'But you're much more important than the keys, you know. The most important thing of all, is for you to be good and honest and truthful. Mmm?'

Another nod.

'And you know it's wrong to steal, don't you? And wrong to tell lies?'

Silence.

'Tom?'

Thomas gulped suddenly, beamed and wriggled free of his father's hands. 'I forgot,' he said. 'But I've remembered now.'

He ran across to the high chair, rummaged under the plastic seat cover and pulled out a bunch of keys. 'I was playing burglars, and I put them under here. For the shop.'

Nick closed his eyes for a second and breathed very, very slowly. Just in case someone asked about the burglar game.

But no one was concerned with that. Mr Fisher was still watching Thomas with that solemn look.

'No, Tom, that won't do. You didn't forget. You knew all the time, and you were lying to us.'

Nick could hardly believe his ears. 'For heaven's sake, he's only a kid. What do you expect?'

For a second all three of them were looking at him, Mr and Mrs Fisher and Ruth, all staring as though he'd said something out of turn. Then Mrs Fisher patted his shoulder and scooped up an armful of bank bags. 'Will you help me to put these in the safe, Nick?'

It was obvious why she'd said it. She was getting him out of the way, so that Mr Fisher could deal with Thomas uninterrupted. Oh well, if that was what they wanted, why should he interfere? Nick scooped up the rest of the bags and followed her into the store-room behind the shop.

It was only when she opened the battered cupboard door and he saw the safe hidden inside that he realized what had happened.

# Chapter 14

It froze in front of his eyes like a photograph. The shabby, green-painted safe standing on the floor of the cupboard, and Mrs Fisher kneeling down to ladle in the money bags.

He knew it all now. How the burglar alarm worked, where the keys and the money were kept, and when the money went to the bank. The game was over, and it was time to add up the score. He could stop bothering about the Fishers and go straight back to Terry, with the quest completed and his hand held out for the ten pounds.

If that was what he wanted.

'Is that all?' Mrs Fisher said.

Nick blinked down at her. 'What?'

'Is that all the money? Or is there some left in the kitchen?' Mrs Fisher looked up at him questioningly. 'Are you all right, Nick?'

For a moment he wondered what she would say if he answered her. *Actually, I'm just deciding whether your shop will be burgled or not.* But then he knew. She would stay there, just as she was, on her knees, and listen to him. Because the choice he had to make was the sort of choice the Fishers understood.

He didn't say anything. He just pushed the money bags at her and backed out fast, with the whole business churning round in his head. He was in such a hurry that he crashed into Joseph who was coming down the stairs.

'Watch who you're charging,' Joseph said. 'I'm an invalid, you know.' As if to prove it, he was caught by a fit of coughing, leaning sideways against the kitchen door-post.

Nick's mind was so full of other things that he could hardly take in the meaning of the words. 'You're ill?'

'Dying,' Joseph said cheerfully. 'Afraid of catching the dreaded cold?'

Nick mumbled something indistinct. It sounded peculiar to him, but Joseph didn't seem to notice. 'Dad's putting

Tom to bed,' he said, 'so I can do your puncture while Ruth gets ready for the game. All right?'

'Fine,' Nick said vaguely.

Joseph went into the kitchen, opened one of the battered cupboards, and took out a puncture kit. 'I like mending punctures. Very satisfying.' He grinned at Nick. 'And I need to be good at it, with my bike.'

It was Nick's own joke, but all he could manage was a feeble grin. 'I'll come and hold the torch for you, shall I?'

He hoped it would take his mind off other things, but of course it was useless. Joseph bent over the bike and Nick had nothing to do except keep the torch steady, and think. About safes and keys and choosing.

It was ridiculous to be in a state like this. He could have ten pounds, just for the asking. And it wasn't as though Joseph or Ruth would ever know what he'd done. Why was he hesitating?

He watched Joseph's hands working on the inner tube, steadily and efficiently. Watched his solemn face. It reminded him of the way the other Fishers had looked at Thomas. Concentrating.

'Fisher—'

'Got it!' Joseph grinned over his shoulder as he spotted the little trail of bubbles in the bowl of water. Then he turned away to sneeze, and Nick stepped forward. 'Keep the light still.'

*Leave it alone*, said a voice in Nick's head. *Thomas has got nothing to do with you.* But he couldn't leave it alone.

'Joe—you know the keys were lost?'

Joseph marked round the hole and started to sort out a patch. 'We ought to find a better place to keep those keys. Thomas and Susie aren't really old enough to understand how important they are.'

'That's not what your dad thought. He really put the kid through it. Talked about lying and stealing.'

'But he—' Joseph was stopped by a cough. He pulled a face. 'Sorry.'

'But he what?' It would have been easier to let it go, but Nick's brain went back to it, like a tongue going back to a mouth ulcer. 'Don't you think he was being too tough on Thomas?'

The rubber solution oozed out of the tube on to the tyre and Joseph spread it carefully. Then he said, 'So what do you think he should have done?'

'Oh, I dunno.' Nick thought for a moment, wondering how his own father would have behaved. 'Shouted a bit, perhaps. But not gone all *serious* like that.'

Joseph sat back on his heels. His eyes were red and his nose was swollen and he didn't look as though he were enjoying the conversation, but Nick could see him hunting for the right words to explain. 'But it was serious,' he said at last. 'You can't say that stealing's all right before you're eight—or ten, or whatever. If it's wrong, it's always wrong.'

Nick frowned. 'But he's only—what? Four? It can't really *matter*.'

'You can't say that.' Joseph shook his head. 'If you say it doesn't matter what Thomas does, that's like saying *Thomas* doesn't matter. Dad took the trouble to tell him off because he cares about him.'

It was like a slap round the face. Nick snapped back, without thinking. 'So you're training him to be a saint, are you?'

And somewhere, under the anger, he knew what he wanted Joseph to answer. Crazily, insanely, he wanted him to say, *Yes. Only saints have to bother with being as good as that.* Because somehow, in a way that he didn't even understand, that would be the solution to his own problem.

But Joseph didn't say anything of the kind. 'A saint? What are you talking about? You don't understand anything, do you?' His voice was almost rough. 'Why don't you just keep that torch straight? I can't see in the dark, you know.'

Nick held the torch beam steady and shut up.

That was all, they hadn't even quarrelled properly, but something between them was jangled. They didn't speak for the next few minutes, until Joseph had finished mending the puncture. Then, as he put everything away into the tin, all he said was, 'The game?'

Nick nodded, but it wasn't right, and they both knew it. And the feeling from their argument seemed to have spread, to have infected everything around them, far worse than any cold virus could have done. The whole air of the house was wrong as they went in and there was something bleak and chilly about the deserted kitchen.

As they climbed the stairs they could hear Mr and Mrs Fisher talking in the bathroom while they got Thomas ready for bed. Mr Fisher was being bright and brisk and chattering too much, but Mrs Fisher sounded like a zombie. Every word she spoke fell with a thud. Joseph didn't look round, but Nick saw his nails dig into the palms of his hands. *Wrong*, said a whisper in his head. *It's all wrong*. When Ruth called out for them to come into the bedroom, he felt like running down the stairs instead.

But he was through the door before he had made his mind up and suddenly it was too late. He felt his way along the wall in the dark and sat down in his usual place on the bed. Then he slid his fingers round the little hard shape of the Star Warrior, pulled it out of his pocket and stood it on the stool.

Joseph took a few moments to arrange his things, fumbling slightly as though his cold made him tired. But at last he nodded. 'Go on, start it off.'

Nick stared through the darkness at the black silhouette that was Ruth, motionless on her chair. Even she seemed different today. The heap of hair on her head was twisted into smooth curves that might have been carved out of wood, and locks fell down on either side of her neck, disguising the shape of her head. For a second, Nick had the terrifying feeling that he was about to speak to a pagan image, not made in any human shape. Something that hid in darkness because it was too ugly for people to endure.

Beside him, Joseph snuffled suddenly and that changed into horror as well. Suppose that wasn't human breathing. Suppose—

He was being stupid. The sensible thing would be to get the game going. Then the torch would go on and he would be able to see Joseph, at least. Taking a deep breath, Nick spoke into the darkness.

'We are here, O Queen, ready to continue our journey.'

His voice came out very strong and fierce, surprising even himself, and it was an instant or two before Ruth answered. But when she did, they were straight into the game.

'You are standing at the foot of the secret staircase which the Nightwalker showed you?'

Nick felt a small, ridiculous flicker of relief that her voice was unchanged. 'We are.'

'Then you must make a choice,' Ruth said softly. 'Because the way divides. There are two tunnels which lead from the foot of the stairs.'

Nick and Joseph both sat up straighter, listening hard, and Joseph switched on the torch, holding his pen ready. Ruth breathed once, quietly, before she went on.

'The tunnel on the left is high and smooth-walled, lit by flaming torches on either side. After a hundred paces or so, it bends round to the left, and the rest of it is hidden.'

'And the tunnel on the right?' said Nick.

'Darker. Lower and narrower.' Ruth paused again. 'And there is no light except the light from your own torch. But by that light you can see cracks running down the walls of the tunnel and across the floor.'

'What sort of cracks?' Nick tried to imagine it.

'As if—'

Ruth hesitated and Joseph suddenly went very still, but Nick didn't guess what was coming. 'As if what?'

She waited a second more, and then the words came out in a strong, firm voice. 'As if the ground is unstable there. As if it shifts.'

'No,' Joseph said, loudly and hoarsely. He put down his pen. 'No, Ruth, you're mad. We can't play *that*.'

# Chapter 15

For a second nobody spoke, but the air was full of struggle. Nick could feel the two of them facing each other across the room, knew that they were both sitting stiff and upright, glaring through the darkness.

'It's only a game,' he said at last. 'What's the fuss?'

Joseph's voice came through clenched teeth. '*She* knows.'

'But we don't even have to take that way if you don't want to.' Nick still didn't understand why Joseph was upset. So Ruth had used the shifting ground that caused them all problems. What was wicked about that? If she knew Joseph was going to throw a tantrum, it was dead clever, in fact. Nick was certain that the shifting tunnel was the one they should take. The other one was so pleasant that it was sure to be hiding a crew of monsters and no treasure. He needed to talk Joseph round.

But he didn't get a chance, because Joseph suddenly stood up and spoke directly to Ruth, outside the game.

'I don't know what you're up to, but it's—it's indecent. Don't you realize what's going to happen to our family if we can't get out of this place? And you know what's keeping us here as well as I do. Give up, Ruth. Take it back, or I'm walking out of the game.'

Useless. Pointless. Nick felt like giving him a good shake. Even he knew that Ruth was not the sort of person who ever backed down. Now he'd put it like that, she wouldn't compromise, not in a million years. She was sitting rigidly still on her chair, remote as a carved image, and Nick could feel the strength of the cold fury that came from her.

Then, all at once, she was on her feet, moving quickly towards the wardrobe. Before Nick even realized what was happening, the wardrobe door creaked as she put her hand on it and the game was on the verge of cracking apart.

'No. Stop.' He gabbled the words, because he knew that once she had vanished there would be no summoning her again. 'Forget about Joseph—about Jethro. He can stay where he is if he wants to. I'm going on alone.'

There was total stillness. Ruth didn't move or speak. But she didn't disappear into the wardrobe, either. She simply waited where she was and at last Nick got it. Joseph had broken the game, had spoken to her by her own name about their own family. Something had to happen to repair that breach.

'Oh come on, Fisher.' Nick tried not to sound too annoyed. 'Think what it's like for me. I've come all this way and I've got a long ride home to look forward to. Are you telling me I don't even get a game?'

Nothing. Silence.

'Let me go by myself. Take half an hour out if you like.' *Or get out altogether and let me play solo with Ruth.* Nick skipped the last bit, but it was there, ready to explode out of him if Joseph went on behaving like an idiot.

'I don't—' Joseph said slowly. He didn't finish, but pushed the map and his pen towards Nick, indicating that he was on his own now. Then he sat back, with his hands folded on his knees.

*OK, be like that, then. I'll manage fine without you. Fine.* Nick grabbed the map, smoothed it out and marked in the two tunnels as carefully as he could, trying not to notice how wobbly and uncertain his lines looked beside Joseph's neat ones.

'I am here,' he said, when he'd got the map up to date. No point in getting into another argument. He was just going to assume that it was all right and that Ruth would go on playing. 'I am here, O Queen, waiting at the fork to choose which tunnel to take.'

She rustled slowly across the room and settled herself in her chair. Beside Nick, Joseph was motionless, waiting.

'Which tunnel do you take, Zephaniah?' she said softly, at last.

The solution was obvious. To stop Joseph throwing another fit he ought to take the light, bright one, without the cracks. And that was what he had intended to do. But suddenly, with a quick, sharp spurt of anger, he changed his mind. You couldn't play a game like this unless you

100

played it properly, and he was *sure* the light tunnel was the wrong one. If Joseph didn't like what he did, then let him get out.

'I'm taking the dark tunnel. The one with the cracks.'

There was no reaction from Joseph, but Ruth took a long, slow breath and Nick knew suddenly that she had double-bluffed him. Whatever the trap was, he was walking straight into it, on his own, and that was exactly what she had intended. But it was too late to back out now.

'I take the torch from Jethro and walk into the tunnel,' he said evenly, and with one finger he pushed the Star Warrior along the top of the stool, until it was standing a couple of inches away from the dwarf. Then he waited for Ruth to go on.

Her voice didn't give him any more clues. 'The ground is rough, broken by the cracks, but they are narrow enough for you to jump easily. Under your feet there is a slight stickiness—'

'Mud?'

'Not mud. Not anything you recognize. As you come round the first corner, you see long, ragged strands hanging from the walls and ceiling of the tunnel.'

Nick tried to visualize it. 'What sort of strands?'

'As thick as rope, but not rope. They're a dull grey, and their surface is sticky, so that they cling to each other where they touch. But any pattern they made has been broken.'

He ought to be able to work out what was going on. Her words meant something more, something that he could work out if only he put the clues together right. He tried to push his brain, to solve it, but all he could think of was the shifting ground and the broken rocks.

'I examine the walls and the ceiling very carefully. Are they safe? Are there any loose rocks?'

The black shape of Ruth's head moved against the strip of dull grey sky. 'Nothing loose. The tunnel is cracked, but it's perfectly sound.'

'All right, I'll go on then. But I'm very careful not to touch the sticky strands.'

'You come to a right-hand bend. A right angle.'

'I go round the corner,' Nick said.

Ruth stood up. Slowly she walked across the room towards him, until she was standing on the other side of the stool. Her face was still in darkness, because of the way the torch was angled, but Nick could see the long green folds of her satin skirt and smell the faint incense scent that clung to it.

His whole body was tensed up, because now it was Ruth herself who had broken out of the game. It was role-playing, fantasy, all-in-the-head stuff—only now suddenly there she was in person, with her Jezebel clothes and her strange scent. He leaned back, with his heart thudding against his ribs, because he had no idea what to expect now. Was she going to hit him on the head? Throw something into his face? It could be anything at all.

'The air is thick,' she murmured, and her voice was only just loud enough to carry across the stool between them. 'Even with the torch you see dimly. But you can make out that the tunnel ends in a smooth rock wall. And the centre of that wall is a huge door, also made of rock.'

She bent down slightly to place something on the table, right in front of the Star Warrior. Only her hand moved into the patch of light. It was loaded with rings, bits of twisted metal set with coloured glass that glinted as they moved. Neatly, precisely, the ringed fingers set a large matchbox on its edge to block the Star Warrior's path.

The stone door.

It was a challenge, no doubt about that. Ruth hadn't dreamt up the stone door and put it actually, physically in front of him unless there was something important behind it. A written message or a talisman perhaps? But it could be a model of her own, a monster or an evil magician or something. Nick stared at the matchbox and it loomed huge and solid, so that he was seeing it as if he really was Zephaniah, with a decision to make.

So what would Zephaniah do? Not strong, not clever, not brave except for thinking God was on his side—it was pretty obvious what he'd do, wasn't it? He'd turn meekly round and go back to take the other tunnel. Only—

'Can I open the door?' he said.

'You can try.' There was no clue in Ruth's voice (was

102

there ever?) but at least she wasn't stopping him.

'I put my hands against the stone and push it as hard as I can.' He wondered whether she meant him to touch the matchbox, but decided against it. Instead, he imagined the Star Warrior with his arms raised, heaving at the rock with all his strength (*all*—ha ha).

'You can't move it.'

No great surprise about that. 'Can I slide it?'

'No.'

'How about a Spell of Opening?'

No answer. Fine. That meant, *Give it a whirl, if you dare*, which was a good sign. Desperately Nick tried to remember one of the spells he had read in Joseph's exercise book. He hadn't bothered to memorize them properly because he had never expected to be stuck on his own like this, and for a second he glanced sideways at Joseph, wondering if he could ask for a clue. But that would be cheating. And anyway, Joseph was looking away, down at his hands, as though he had somehow shut his mind to what was going on.

There had to be a spell lurking somewhere in his head. What was the peculiar one that had the little crocodiles drawn underneath it? *By the cucumbers* . . . He launched out on it and the words came into his mouth as he needed them.

'By the cucumbers of Egypt,
By the rivers of Babylon,
By the seven-chambered temple of the priests
of Ashtaroth,
I charge you to open to me.'

For an instant he thought that it wasn't going to work. That he would be stuck, with the tunnel blocked off and the rock wall rising solid in front of him. Then Ruth reached out giant hands towards the door, one to hold it and the other, with an outstretched finger, to push the centre section out. She was not swinging the whole thing away as he had expected. She was opening the matchbox.

It moved very slowly, grating like rock against rock, and Nick held his breath. Half of him was outside the fantasy, knowing that there would be nothing to see except the inside of a matchbox with a bit of paper or plastic; but the other half of him was Zephaniah, the Star Warrior, waiting with no weapon but a slingshot and his bare hands. Ready for action, with the adrenalin pumping into his bloodstream.

The huge door slid, and through the gap—the instant that there was any gap at all—black legs scrabbled a way out.

*Legs?*

He had scaled down. They were huge legs, four feet long and six inches thick, with hairs sprouting from the surface. *Moving.* He nearly shrieked aloud with the shock of it, but he managed to get a grip on himself in time. It had to be a joke, a fake. One of those things kids buy to give their mothers a heart attack. It had to be.

It was real.

A spider as big as the Star Warrior, scuttling out of the box towards him, huge legs moving all at once, head poised.

Ruth rapped suddenly on the stool, with one ringed finger, and the spider froze, half an inch from the little figure, as if it were ready for battle. Nick felt frozen too, trapped somewhere in between fantasy and reality.

Then Ruth spat out one word. 'Venom!'

OK, it was a monster. No point in rolling dice against it. It would be all over Zephaniah before the numbers were added. And anyway, this was no ordinary test, not the way Ruth had set it up. Nick's body shrank away from the spider automatically, but he reckoned that that was what it was all about. Ruth was daring him, trying to show him up as some kind of squeamish idiot. Well, she was going to fail.

Quite coldly and deliberately, he shoved out his hand and brought it down hard on the spider. It scuttled as he moved, but his aim was as good as it had always been. His palm smacked down on the wood, there was a tiny squelch and—that was that. Not half as bad as he had expected. *Got you, Jezebel! And I'd better score some good points for that, or I'll want to know the reason why.*

He wasn't exactly expecting cheers, but he thought one of them might have said something or chuckled or let him know he'd scored. Instead, there was total, dead silence.

Then Joseph said, '*Ruth!*'

'*He* did it, not me.' It was Ruth's own voice, brisk and unceremonious. 'It was his decision. I just gave him the chance to make the choice. That's what this game's about, isn't it?'

'Great, absolutely great!' Joseph shouted. 'I bet the spider thought it was really worth while.'

Nick's brain moved slowly into a different key. They weren't even arguing about whether he'd made the right move or the wrong one, only about whether it was his fault. As if there was no question.

'For heaven's sake!' He added his bit to the yelling. 'It was only a spider. You're not going to tell me you've never killed a spider, are you?'

Silence. The kind of silence where no one needs to spell anything out because the *Yes* is humming in the air.

'If you feel like that, why aren't you bloody vegetarians?'

'We are,' Ruth said, in a small, tight voice.

That was *it*. Nick grabbed the Star Warrior and jumped up, yelling at them. 'OK, so you're too holy to live! Well, be like that. Stay here and let the monsters crawl all over you. Let your house come crashing down without trying to save yourselves because it's *stealing*. I'm a fighter. I look after myself. And I'm getting out!'

He raced for the doorway, rubbing his spidery hand on Joseph's hair as he passed. As he pushed through the door, he banged his shins on the edge. It was agony, but he just kept going, across the landing and down the stairs.

When he pushed open the kitchen door, there was Mr Fisher still at the table, with the bills spread out in front of him. He was staring down at them with a grey face and rubbing his hand slowly up and down his chin.

Too bad! If the Fishers were hard up, it was their own look-out. Nick didn't want to think about it. He'd *had* the Fisher family.

Loudly—purposely loudly—he crashed through the kitchen to the back door, watching with satisfaction as Mr Fisher raised his head and blinked. Then he was out in the night, on his own.

Somehow, at the back of his head, he expected to feel

better once he was in the cold and the dark, with nobody watching him. But the ride only made his anger fiercer. The wind across the Marsh whipped at his face, coming harder than he was ready for. No thrashing trees to warn him, no rustling hedges. Only the brutal wind and the treacherous, shifting ground. He cycled with his teeth clenched and his face screwed up with determination.

By the time he got home, there was nothing in his mind except fury. Without thinking, like a machine, he climbed the stairs and knocked on Terry's door.

'Yes?'

Nick pushed the door open. 'You know those questions you gave me? For the quest?'

'Well?' Terry sat up sharply.

'I've come to tell you the answers.'

# Chapter 16

'We-ell now,' Terry said, very slow, so that Nick knew he was surprised, that he hadn't really expected to get the information. 'Come across. Have a seat on the bed and I'll see if I've got ten pounds.'

He was trying to sound cool and casual, but his voice shook with excitement.

'I don't want ten pounds,' Nick said stiffly. Quite out of the blue, he knew that ten pounds wasn't enough to make up for what he had been through. He wanted something more. Much more.

Terry's eyes snapped, watching him hard. 'What *do* you want, then?'

Nick drew a deep breath. 'I want to come with you.'

'You want—you're crazy!' It was an automatic response, exploding before Terry could catch himself. 'Come where? What are you talking about?'

'Don't put me off.' Nick walked across the room. 'I'm not a little kid that you can tell fairy stories to. I know what you do when you go out with your mates. And so do Mum and Dad, only they won't admit it.'

Terry looked at him silently, as if he could choke him off by not answering at all. But Nick went on, deliberately. There was a kind of thrill in speaking the words, as if he were slashing at something fragile and precious.

'I want to come with you and the others when you wreck the Fishers' shop.'

He saw Terry's throat move as he swallowed, watched his face grow paler, as if he had had a physical shock, and he punched home his advantage.

'It's no good pretending. I know. I saw you riding off last time, leaving the road and cutting across the fields. I even know you've got room for me because no one rides pillion on your bike.'

Terry swallowed again and then, all at once, he came to life. 'Right then, let's have it. You prove you've got what

107

we want to know, and I'll swing it for you to come with us. But if you don't keep your mouth shut afterwards—'

'Of course I'll keep my mouth shut. I'll be in it, won't I, just the same as you?'

Slowly Terry nodded and Nick sat down on the mattress beside him. For a second they looked at each other, without speaking. Terry's head was very still against the black background of his bedroom wall, and suddenly Nick felt the familiar thrill of an adventure about to start. But this time it was real.

*Faces looking at each other in the torchlight, with darkness and danger everywhere around. Comrades, ready for the adventure.*

He looked down at his hands and began to talk, steadily and quietly. 'We've got to do it tomorrow. That's the day before they bank the money, when it's all in the safe. And the whole lot of them go off to their gran's for the evening. They even take the little ones . . .'

He said it all, just as he had rehearsed it in his head while he was cycling home. Quite coolly, he listened to his voice going on and on, giving the information, answering Terry's questions and making arrangements. And he felt quite calm, as if they were planning a picnic or a visit to the cinema. He could see that Terry was impressed, because he looked at him with a different expression, as if Nick had suddenly grown five years older.

When it was all settled, Nick stood up, nodded to Terry and walked out of the room, down the landing to his bedroom. Still calm, still detached. As he switched the light on, his reflection stared back at him from the mirror on the opposite wall. The same face, but subtly altered. In earnest, as if he had stepped across a divide into the real, adult world. He suddenly felt reckless and wild.

It was a strange, new feeling. As though Good and Bad—those two old bogeymen—had vanished like fairy tales. He could simply do whatever he chose, without worrying about them. It was a splendid, exhilarating feeling, but frightening as well, as if he were riding a roller coaster that was almost out of control. Defiantly he blacked out the fear with triumph.

*I'm going to ride with The Company.*

On Tuesday morning, they had cookery. Nick and Livingstone stood side by side at a kitchen table chopping onions for a stew. Behind them, they could hear Sharon Wilson scolding Parker.

'Stop putting bits in your mouth. It's unhygienic. Honestly, Parker, you're the only person in the class who'd eat *raw onion*.'

Livingstone grinned at Nick. 'Isn't it nice what simple lives some people lead? Nothing worse to worry about than eating raw onion.'

Nick grinned back. That was just what he wanted today—ordinary school talk, with nothing in it about the Fishers or shops or bikes. 'Pretty easy way to rebel and live a wild life. Just shove a bit of onion in your mouth and breathe all over squeaky-clean old Sharon.'

They didn't need to discuss it. At the same second, they both took a mouthful of onion and chewed hard.

'Right,' said Livingstone. 'Now!'

Both of them whirled round and opened their mouths. Sharon staggered back as the onion fumes hit her. 'You're all revolting. I don't know why I can't cook with someone decent!'

Mrs Maloney looked over her shoulder. 'Sharon! Stop making so much noise!'

Sharon subsided, pulling a face at all three of them, and Livingstone shook his head with mock sadness as he and Nick turned back to their onions. 'It's so easy to get into trouble if you don't take care.'

He reached for his knife and glanced sideways at Nick, but he didn't say anything straight away. Instead, he chopped quickly and carefully, making neat, even slices. When all his onions were ready, he unwrapped his piece of meat and spread it out on the chopping board. Then he spoke, very softly, without looking up.

'Talking of getting into trouble—what happened about Joseph Fisher? Did anything come of that?'

Nick gulped, taken by surprise. 'What do you mean?'

'Oh, come on,' Livingstone said lightly. 'You must have guessed I was in on it. Just for a laugh.'

'I thought—you might be.'

Livingstone sliced neatly into the meat, cutting out a streak of gristle that ran through the middle. 'So what happened? Or are you going to sulk because I played a trick on you?'

'Not sulking—' Nick hesitated for a second. He wasn't even angry now. Instead, he felt a fierce burst of happiness, because Livingstone didn't know what was going on. *He* wasn't one of The Company. *He* wasn't going to ride out on an adventure. For once he was one up on Livingstone.

Only he couldn't tell him. Because that went with being one of The Company. Secrecy. Loyalty.

Carefully, Nick undid the bloodstained parcel that held his own piece of meat. 'I'd have thumped you if I'd known it was you in the beginning. But it's all turned out OK. I've got quite friendly with Fisher.'

He was avoiding the question, and they both knew it, but Livingstone wasn't the sort of person to push things. He just raised an eyebrow and gave a small, tight smile.

'Well, I guess you're better off not getting mixed up with Donna's friends. Danger's not really your scene, is it?'

*Danger.*

Nick closed his eyes for a second and then cut down, hard, into the raw meat.


By the evening, he was so strung up that he could hardly breathe. Now. It had to be now. He didn't know if he was excited or afraid but he felt as though he would explode if something didn't happen soon.

And then it was half-past eight and Terry pushed the door open. 'They're here. Come on.'

'I—'

It was only a brief hesitation, but Terry was on to it at once. He crossed the bedroom in two strides and grabbed Nick's arm. 'Come on. No time to hang around.'

Nick took a deep breath and stood up. *Here we go.* Now that it was really beginning he found that he could behave calmly. He even managed to smile at his mother as they passed her in the hall.

'Just going out for a ride with Terry, Mum. Won't be long.'

He saw her frown, as if she were trying to work out whether that would keep Terry safe or put Nick in danger. But before she got her answer they were through the front door, in the dark.

The others were together, under the lamp-post, straddling their bikes and looking towards the house. Donna on her big Honda, Bill with his battered helmet swinging in one hand, and Leo smiling at some private joke.

The moment Nick walked through the front gate, he knew they were expecting him. Their heads turned and Bill jerked a thumb.

'Over here, kid.'

Terry gave Nick a push between the shoulder-blades. 'Go on.'

Awkwardly Nick moved into the centre of the group and Bill looked him up and down, as if he were examining a bike he might buy. Then he nodded and looked round at the others. 'What d'you think? Shall we let him come?'

For a second Nick saw the circle of faces under the lamplight, all watching him. Leo gave him a quick wink and Donna scowled. Then Leo said, 'Why not? Might make things a bit more amusing.'

Bill looked at Donna. 'What about you, Don? He's not coming unless we all agree. Same rules as usual.'

Donna shrugged. 'Bit late to say no now, isn't it? The kid knows what's going on.'

'He'll shut up whatever happens. Won't you?' Bill gave Nick a smile that wasn't kind or amused. 'Come on, Don. Don't keep us hanging about.'

Nick was afraid that Donna was going to send him inside again, like a little child that has to be left with his parents. But in the end she nodded sulkily and Bill put a hand on Nick's shoulder.

'Same rules for you. You don't come unless you've chosen it yourself, of your own free will. And if you're with us, you *stick* with us. Because we're all in it together. OK?'

Nick had to fight to keep the grin of happiness off his face. 'OK.'

Bill smiled again and pointed backwards. 'Come up on the back of my bike.'

Too late to argue or to say that he wanted to ride with Terry. Nick took the spare helmet that Terry was holding out and buckled it on, shutting out everything except the sight of Bill's black leather jacket in front of him.

There was a stutter of engines and a roar as the bikes started together, and then they were moving down the road towards the darkness of the Marsh.

They must have planned it all out carefully, and learned the route, because there was no dawdling around to look at signposts. Straight out over the Marsh they went. They took a jink round Holney Fen, and then they were out into the real dark, where all the lamp-posts stopped and the house windows were just a scatter of lighted squares, somewhere across the mud. Right, left, left, right—they took the turns so fast that Nick could hardly keep track of them.

And all the time, he was wedged against Bill's back, with the wind ballooning their jackets as they leaned into the curves together. The cold air smacked against the side of his face as they turned—right, left, right, left—and fear stamped around in his stomach.

It was the most exciting thing he had ever felt. *This is real, a real adventure. There's no one to bale us out. No one to pick us up and kiss it better if it all goes wrong. We're out on our own.* He and Joseph had played at it, this was the real thing. They were racing into danger with no one to rely on but each other. Comrades. Warriors.

The village nameplate flashed suddenly in the head-lights—*Holney Seas End*—and the next instant, they were pulling up outside the shop. The moment the engines died, Donna started to scream.

'You moron! Where's this? This isn't where my nan lives!'

'Knock it off, Michelle,' Terry yelled back at her, just as loud. 'How do you expect me to tell the difference between these crummy villages?'

Bill took off his helmet and turned to Nick. 'Come on,' he said, so softly that Nick hardly heard him. 'Keys in the kitchen. Right?'

Nick removed his own helmet and slid off the bike as Bill

112

wheeled it round the far side of the shop, away from the kitchen entrance. In a second or two, the bike was hidden in the ditch which separated the shop's forecourt from the first field. Then Nick and Bill slipped round the back and into the yard, through the double gates. The others were still yelling at the tops of their voices. Decoys? It seemed a risky way to do it.

'Won't they just attract attention to us?' he hissed in Bill's ear.

'Do *you* know anyone who'd come out in the dark to deal with a crowd of quarrelling bikers?' Bill said scornfully. 'They'll watch through their windows and when the others go off, they'll heave a sigh of relief and settle back to watch their televisions. You wait and see. No one's going to trouble us until we've finished with this little lot.'

He leaned on the back door and Nick heard something scrape against the wood. Then Bill gave a grunt and there was a splintering sound. Not loud. If Nick had been ten metres further away, he wouldn't have heard it at all, because out in the road the bikes roared suddenly. A second later, the sound of the engines was fading into the distance as the others took off across the Marsh.

The two of them were on their own.

# Chapter 17

'*Very* quiet now,' Bill murmured in his ear. 'This is the tricky bit.' He grabbed Nick's arm and pushed him forwards, into the kitchen. 'You know where the keys are. You go in and get them.'

*This is it,* said a voice in Nick's head. *This is where you take the risk and find out if you're brave or not.*

But it wasn't like that. It was cold, mechanical, as if he had no option. Three quick steps across the kitchen to the big kitchen table. No need to trouble with the light. Even in the dark he could feel along the smooth, painted edge of the wood to find the corner of the drawer. His fingers moved to the wooden handle, pulled the drawer half open and snaked inside.

The keys were the first thing they touched. A leather tag and a bunch of cold metal keys, just ready to be picked up, as if God had put them there for him.

Well, maybe . . .

Bill was there instantly, reaching out for them. 'Right, take me to the shop door,' he hissed in Nick's ear. He sounded brisk and hostile, more like a stranger than a comrade.

Through the kitchen door into the little lobby at the bottom of the stairs. It was dark there, but Nick couldn't remember how to find the light switch. Instead, he pushed Bill towards the shop door.

'That one,' he muttered. 'There's a lock halfway up and—'

'Yes,' Bill snapped. For the first time Nick realized how strung up he was. 'Move.'

There was almost time to cool down and think then. Bill had to try all the keys, one after the other, to turn off the burglar alarm at the top of the door. Then he had to try them all over again to unlock the door. Nick heard him breathing, fast and shallow.

And Bill wasn't the only one. Inside Terry's second-best

114

leather jacket, Nick felt the sweat, clammy in his armpits, as the house creaked. Oh sure, it was an old house and old houses always creaked, especially if they were cracked through the foundations. But it sounded like someone moving overhead, turning in a bed or rocking a chair.

Nick kept imagining footsteps on the stairs. The sort of footsteps you imagine when you're lying in bed and thinking that there might be a burglar in the house. And then he thought, *But I'm the burglar*, and he had to push his fist into his mouth to keep back a shout of nervous laughter.

Bill shoved the door suddenly, and it swung open, without a sound. Nick heard him start to breathe more easily as they stepped in and pulled the door almost shut.

'OK. Where's the safe then?' Bill took a small flashlight out of his pocket and shone it round, over the sacks of potatoes and the heaps of brown cardboard boxes.

'Over there, behind that stack,' Nick said. 'It's in the cupboard.'

Bill was there in two strides, wrenching the cupboard door open to reveal the battered green safe. Coolly, he spread the keys on the palm of his hand and studied them and then he selected one and pushed it into the keyhole.

'Bingo,' he said softly. 'Got it first time.'

There it was. A little pile of bank bags full of different coins, a bank paying-in book and two bundles of paper.

Bill picked up the thinner bundle, spat and tore the cheques in half before he flung them back into the safe. Then he took the bigger bundle and flicked the notes through his fingers.

'You sure this is a whole week's money?'

'Well, Joseph said—'

'OK, OK.' Bill shoved the notes into his pocket, grabbed up the bank bags and jerked his head towards the shop. Then he shone the light down at his watch. 'Open up. I think we'll let the others in now.' He held out the keys.

'But I thought—'

'Don't. Just do what you're told. Fast.'

Nick took the keys and walked through the dark shop, picking up the smells that were already so familiar. Paraffin, cabbages and parsnips, soap powder . . . With his heart thumping, he reached up to unlock the burglar alarm, fumbling along the top of the door-frame until he located the smooth metal of the keyhole. Then he found the ordinary front-door key and turned that in the ordinary lock.

He pushed the door open and stood for a few seconds looking out. It was all very dark, very still. Then, somewhere across the Marsh, a church bell sounded once, distant and lonely, marking half-past nine.

Immediately, as if that were the signal, he heard the bikes start up about half a mile away. They came into the village at top speed and Terry, Leo and Donna exploded into the shop before Nick had time to work out what was happening. Before anyone listening from further up the village could have guessed it wasn't going to be just another quarrel.

Nick fell back as they burst in, pushed aside by the sheer number and size of them. No nonsense about secrecy now. Bill was flicking his torch from shelf to shelf, directing them, finding things for them to wreck, and they were yelling and screaming at the tops of their voices.

Terry swept a shelf of jars to the ground, crunching the glass into the lino. Leo grabbed at the tins. Fast and accurate as a machine-gun, he fired them at the windows at the front of the shop, one and one and one and one and— until the reinforced glass gave way and cracked outwards. And Donna—

It took Nick a second or two to notice what Donna was up to, because she wasn't making any noise. She had fetched two paraffin cans from the store-room and, while the others were screeching and smashing, she was walking round the shop very slowly and methodically sprinkling everything with paraffin.

It all happened at once, in the space of a minute or so. They must have done it so often before that they had worked out how to make the most mess in the shortest time. And all Nick could do was gasp and step back into the far corner of the shop, out of the way.

Then Bill saw what Donna was doing. He grabbed at the paraffin cans. 'You crazy? I've told you a million times—'

116

At the same moment, Leo screamed from the back of the shop. 'There's someone coming!'

All of them moved together, as if they'd rehearsed it. Shift! No tripping over the heaps of junk on the floor, no barging in the doorway. They were outside before Nick could blink, and the footsteps that Leo had heard sounded from the bottom of the stairs, too close for Nick to risk running out. Automatically, he ducked down behind a stack of detergent boxes.

As he ducked, he heard the bikes start up outside. Three of them together and Bill's a couple of breaths later. For a second he couldn't believe it, couldn't believe that they were simply going to ride off and leave him behind. Before he had time to realize the truth, the bikes were off, racing out of the village.

It had all happened so fast that he couldn't take it in. Two minutes ago, he had been standing at the door of the shop, staring out into the quiet darkness of the Marsh. Now the shop was wrecked, the bikes were roaring out of the village without him, and someone was coming down the stairs and into the shop. He was trapped.

The shop lights went on and there was Joseph standing at the back, looking round at the chaos, his face pink and swollen from his cold. What had he said? *Not even the little ones escape the weekly visit to Gran's.* And he'd missed it just because he'd got a cold! Nick scowled and shrank as small as he could behind the boxes. Better wait until Joseph turned back to the telephone, to call the police. That would be the moment to escape from the shop.

But Joseph didn't move. He just stood staring round at the wrecked shop and at the safe swinging open behind him. And other people were coming. Nick heard one voice call from the far end of the village, then another and another. *Come on, Fisher. Move it, or I'll get caught by the yokels.* What was the matter? Had Joseph's cold stopped his brain working?

People were getting closer outside now, still at the far end of the village, but running. Nick panicked as he heard their feet on the road and their voices yelling. Should he try and slip out the back way, at once, and take the risk of Joseph

117

seeing him? But before he could decide, Joseph moved. Not backwards to the phone, but across to the shelves just in front of Nick.

It all happened very fast. Joseph came over, reached up to a high shelf and took a box of matches. Peering from his hiding place, Nick saw the hand shake as it closed round the box.

Hurriedly, clumsily, Joseph grabbed a handful of matches out of the box and scraped them down the side. They lit with a hiss and a sudden flare, all at once, and Joseph flung them roughly toward the nearest pool of paraffin, not looking at what he was doing. Then he ran off to the front door before the matches had even landed.

Why on earth—?

For a second, Nick's mind flipped and he simply couldn't understand what he had seen. And then he remembered Ruth's angry face and her abrupt, bitter voice as she climbed out of the car. *It would be stealing from the insurance company.*

She had longed to set fire to the place, but she had chickened out. Because it was *wrong.* Very noble. And he had almost believed that story. Had been impressed, even, to think that there were people with real principles.

Only now Joseph had a chance to start the fire and blame it all on Terry's gang—and he'd grabbed the opportunity with both hands. Not so noble after all.

Nick thought it all out, angrily, while he was scrambling from behind the boxes. But there was no time to work out just how he felt. At any second, the whole place would go up in flames and he was desperate to escape.

But then, as he turned towards the back door, he saw Joseph's matches.

Amazingly—unbelievably—they had all been thrown too hard. Every one had landed on the far side of the pool of paraffin. Nick could see the small brown scorch marks on the lino where they had flared and gone out.

For some reason, that made him doubly angry. So Joseph was out of trouble, was he? It wouldn't have been like that for Donna. If *she'd* thrown the matches, they would have fallen into the paraffin and set the place ablaze. And

Donna—with her first conviction for fire-raising on the records—would have got done good and proper. But precious Joseph Fisher . . .

The voices were nearer to the shop now. Nick heard them calling down the street to Joseph, heard Joseph shouting back, sounding strange and sharp. It was time to go. Time to get himself out of trouble. But—

But.

His hand moved automatically. There was no time to work out what he was doing or why. He just reached out, as Joseph had done, and grabbed a box of matches from the shelf. Pulling out a handful, he lit them—exactly as Joseph had done.

But he didn't throw them. He dropped them, very carefully and deliberately, into the centre of a pool of paraffin. It flared up, scorching the air against his right cheek as he raced for the store-room, making him blink with its brightness. Glancing over his shoulder, he saw the flames run along the trail of paraffin in both directions and he got himself out of the place at top speed, slithering across the kitchen and wrenching the back door open.

As he came out into the yard, he could hear Joseph at the front of the shop, yelling at people to keep clear because the place was going up in flames. But there was no time to think about that. Nick ducked out through the double gates into the back road and made for the ditch where Bill had hidden his bike.

And then the paraffin store at the back went up. Nick was struggling down the ditch and up the far side, not caring if anyone saw him, just desperate to get out of the way of the fire. As he scrabbled his way over the muddy field, crouching low, he could hear the lids of tins popping off, like bombs exploding, and smell the choking smells—scorched fat, charred vegetables, burnt sugar.

The smoke went out towards the sea in a thick column that showed grey against the night sky, and the roaring of the fire almost drowned out the shouting voices and the noise of cars starting up.

There was no chance of saving the shop. He was halfway to Holney Fen before he heard the fire engines, and they took three tries before they found the right road into Holney Seas End. Amazing really, because anyone should have been able to navigate there by the pillar of smoke and the huge red flames that leapt up, forty feet high, when the roof blew off.

# Chapter 18

Every minute, he expected someone to stop him. Grab hold of his arm and ask him why he was staggering along covered in mud. It was caked into his hair and streaked down his face, and there was a long cut on his cheek where he'd caught it on a stone. He knew he must be a peculiar sight.

But it was as though he were invisible. Even the bored lorry driver who stopped in Holney Fen to give him a lift hadn't shown any interest in him. He was so busy talking about his racing pigeons that he hadn't asked Nick a single question. Against all the odds, Nick found himself safely home, lurching up his own garden path.

From somewhere, he found enough energy to get himself round to the back door and into the kitchen. He could hear his parents in the front room, watching television, and he knew that he should have been grateful to sneak in.

But he couldn't manage any more. It had taken him an hour of hard walking to reach Holney Fen and all he wanted was someone to pick him off the floor, hose the mud off him and let him *sleep*. Even his mother would have done. Even his father.

What he got was Terry. The moment the kitchen door clicked shut, Terry was there, racing down the stairs on tiptoe.

'Up. Come on. And belt up, or Mum'll hear us. She nearly went spare when I came home on my own. And I couldn't tell her—'

He was hissing and shaking and half-carrying Nick, all at the same time, hustling him out of the kitchen before their mother could appear and start on the questions. Nick watched his muddy boots being pulled off and thrown into the cupboard under the stairs, and then he let himself be led up to Terry's room.

'Jesus!' Terry said, as Nick slumped on to the bed. 'Just look at you. Jesus *Christ!*'

*He's rattled*, Nick thought vaguely, as if it was all distant.

*He's really rattled.* Terry didn't seem able to speak a sensible word. Just stared at him and swore and shook, as if he'd been shocked out of his mind.

'You left me,' Nick said. The words came out on their own and they weren't what he meant. They had nothing to do with the anger and confusion in his head. 'You just took off and left me.'

'I'll kill him,' Terry said. 'I'll *kill* him! I rode away first, and I swear I didn't know Bill had left you behind. I never even saw until we were halfway home and—' He started to shake worse, too much to speak.

'What's the agony for?' Nick stared at him. '*I'm* angry, because it was me that had to grovel home over the mud, but why should you care?'

Terry shut his eyes and screwed up his fists. 'Because I bloody looked back, didn't I? When we pulled up at the lights on Holney corner, I saw you weren't there, and I grabbed Bill. And he—'

'He what?' He certainly didn't burst into tears. Nick was ready to swear to that.

'He looked over his shoulder and gave me a lousy grin. You know—*dead unlucky, but no use blaming me.* And I turned round and saw this sheet of flames—' Terry stopped, as if he wasn't going to make it to the end of the sentence.

'And you thought I was in the middle of it all, getting barbecued?' Nick didn't know if he was going to laugh or cry. 'You *moron!*'

He wouldn't have believed that Terry cared twopence for him, but there was no way he was putting on the tragedy act. Bill had made him believe Nick was burning up, and he was still white and shaking from the shock. For a moment, just a moment, Nick thought there must be something to being a brother.

Perhaps he could talk to Terry about what he had seen in the shop, after the others had gone.

Then Terry said, 'Donna's a real lunatic. We'll have the police properly on our backs now. Bill ought to have stopped her coming along. He knows she's a firebug.'

The inside of Nick's head went BOOUUMM!!! in slow

motion as everything exploded into nonsense. Terry thought
Donna had started the fire. Joseph thought *he* had started
the fire. And all the time . . . Joseph . . . the police . . .
Ruth . . . Donna being done for fire-raising . . .

Nick was too exhausted to work out what it all added up
to. All he wanted was to get back into his own room and
sleep and sleep and sleep, to blot out the whole rotten mess.

'Nick?' said Terry's voice. 'Nick?'

And there was his face, swimming like a white blob in the
middle of all the confusion, as Nick looked back from the
doorway. A frowning face, wanting something.

Scared.

'I'm OK,' Nick muttered, with his hand on the door
handle. 'And you're OK too, Terry. I won't tell about
Donna, or about anyone else.'

Vaguely he saw Terry's face clear and relax, so he knew
he'd got that right. Then he went. And the moment he got
into his room he began on the total mental blackout. No
thinking, no weighing up what he'd seen.

No maps.


It worked for the rest of the week. The kids at school were
full of the fire, of course. Half of them were whispering
about how it was a miracle no one had been hurt, and the
other half were making sick jokes about smoked bacon and
kippers. But Joseph wasn't in school so Nick was saved
from having to avoid him, and Livingstone was a surprise
ally. Donna must have told him what had happened,
because he didn't want to talk about the fire either. He and
Nick sat around in corners reading *Playboy* and *Motorcycle
News* and got on with normal life.

As if there had never been a fire.

It all went fine until Monday. By Monday, Nick was
beginning to relax, to believe the propaganda voice in his
head that kept saying, *It's all over. You've got away with it.
What happened is nothing to do with you.*

But as he came out of his last class on Monday, flicking
through Livingstone's bundle of dirty pictures, he actually
bumped into Joseph.

123

Crunch. It was like walking into a wall. Not because they hit each other hard, but because of the shock of finding *that* face suddenly up against his own. Every muscle in Nick's body jerked and his stomach heaved.

'Hi,' said Joseph. But blankly, as if his mind was somewhere else.

And suddenly, instantly, at the sound of his voice, Nick was so angry that he couldn't speak. So angry that all he wanted to do was roar and yell and smash out with both fists.

*You let me down. You drew me a map and then tore it up, turned everything into nonsense. I trusted you. I really thought you were—you were—*

It was senseless, the sort of thing there was no point in saying, and Nick shoved both fists hard down into his pockets just to keep them out of the way, because, even in that black blinding rage, he knew it was suicidal to start beating someone up just outside the Head's room.

But as he shoved, Livingstone's pictures caught against the sides of his right pocket, so that he was aware of them again. What happened next had nothing to do with his brain. His fingers and his voice worked on their own.

'Here. Take a look at these.'

Aggressively, he pushed the bundle under Joseph's nose. Spread the pictures in a fan so that Joseph wouldn't make any mistake, would see all the bare flesh and know what he was being shown.

'Here, you don't need to pretend any more, Fisher. You're just like the rest of us, aren't you?'

Joseph looked stupid and blinked at the pictures for a second, taking in how angry Nick was but not what he was doing. Then, suddenly, he got everything into focus and, automatically, flinched and turned his head away.

Nick screamed at him. 'No need to play the *saint* anymore, Fisher. I've sussed you. You're no different from me and the others.'

'Who said I was different?' Joseph sounded choked and his head was still turned away.

'Oh, come on! You really fancied yourself with all that holy stuff, didn't you? Tried to kid us you'd got a direct line

124

to heaven. Well I've got news for you, Fisher. You don't fool me any more.'

Somewhere inside Nick's head, a voice was telling him to knock it off. Saying he was crazy. But there was no way he could stop the words pouring out.

'Stop sneering down your nose at the rest of us and take a look at Livingstone's pictures! Copy your homework! Come into town with me and nick a few things! This is the real world. Come out and make a map of *that*.'

He wanted to stop, but he couldn't, and there was Joseph staring at him, with wide eyes, as if another, wider, crack in the ground had opened up, right under his feet. As if he could see the flames leaping up from the pit and the devils prancing around with pitchforks. He couldn't leave, any more than Nick could stop yelling. They were both trapped in the craziness and the chaos, with no map, no compass, no landmarks.

Even the words flooding out of Nick's mouth weren't really important. All that mattered was that they were staring at each other and the air was full of hurt and fear and anger, and neither of them knew, any more, *who* was angry or hurt or afraid . . .

And then a heavy hand came down on Nick's shoulder. 'Miller.'

Nick shut off. Closed his eyes in relief and gulped for breath, with the Head's hand anchoring him to reality.

She was gabbling on, of course. She snatched the fan of pictures out of his hand, pulled a face and began some sort of spiel about tawdry sexist rubbish, but she could have been singing madrigals for all Nick cared. He was just thankful to have been pulled out of that terrifying, burning spiral of rage.

The Head shook his shoulder. 'Miller. Did you hear what I said?'

'Yes, Mrs Vanderpeer.' The lie was second nature.

'Well?'

Nick just looked, and she gave an impatient sigh. 'I said you should apologize to Joseph. I don't suppose it's any good trying to explain to you *why* he didn't want to look at your pictures. You and he live in different worlds. But at least you can try to respect other people's beliefs.'

'Yes, Mrs Vanderpeer,' Nick said, looking down meekly.

'Even *you* might have realized that this is a particularly cruel time to bait him, in view of what's just happened to his family.'

'Yes, Mrs Vanderpeer.'

'Go on, then.'

Nick made his face absolutely, perfectly blank, got his voice dead level and looked Joseph straight in the eye. 'I'm sorry, Fisher. I won't do it again.'

Joseph gave him back deadpan politeness for deadpan politeness. 'That's all right.'

'And I'm sorry to hear about the shop.'

'That's all right,' Joseph said again, still like a robot.

The Head turned away and vanished into her office, to shred the pictures, and the two of them were left staring at each other. But neither of them spoke. There were so many questions in Nick's head, so many angry, bewildered questions that he simply couldn't begin. And Joseph looked completely blank, shut away behind some invisible wall of his own that cut him off from the rest of the world.

*What does it feel like, being wicked, Fisher?*

Nick didn't ask the question, but even thinking of it drew off all his anger, quite suddenly. He smiled once at Joseph. A small, puzzled, twisted smile. Then he pushed past and went on up the corridor and out of the building.

As he walked slowly towards the bicycle shed, he pushed the whole thing out of his mind and concentrated on inventing something to tell Livingstone, an excuse for losing the pictures. Not that Livingstone would care particularly. He lost his bundle of pictures at least once a term. But thinking about that was better than thinking about anything else.

# Chapter 19

And then he met Donna Livingstone, as he reached the front gate, and everything changed. Donna was dead pale, almost green round the mouth, and so uptight that she could hardly speak. The minute she saw Nick she signalled to him.

'Here, kid. Where's Terry?'

'Lay off.' Nick dodged the hand that was grabbing for his sleeve. 'How should I know? Been at school all day, haven't I?'

Donna looked even sicker. 'I've hammered on the door, but I can't get any answer.'

'Well, he's probably still in bed.' Nick fished out his door key, watching Donna sideways as he did it. 'Want me to go and dig him out for you?'

As they climbed the stairs, she followed so close that Nick could feel her breath on the back of his neck. The moment Terry's door was open a crack, so that they could see him sprawled out on the mattress, Donna shoved Nick inside, stepped in after him, and shut the door.

'Get out of bed,' she snapped at Terry. 'We're in it up to the neck. Bill's gone.'

'What do you mean?' Terry sat up, blinking, still not quite with it, and Donna gripped him by the shoulders and shook him.

'He's gone. Taken off. Hopped it. Some old devil in Holney Seas End took the number of his bike and the police were round his house, but his mum kept them talking while he nipped out the back and—'

Her voice was getting higher and higher and faster and faster. *Donna* was scared. Nick screwed up his fists. The faster she talked, the faster his blood thundered in his ears and the faster he had to breathe to get a bit of air.

'Knock if off, Don!' Terry said sharply. He shook himself free of her hands and stood up. 'You're not trying to tell me that Bill grassed on us? Because I don't believe it.

127

*No one* tells. That's what we've always agreed.'

'Yes, but if they've got Bill's name, it won't take them long to track the rest of us down, will it?' Donna said scornfully. 'They've only got to go into a few pubs, ask a few questions. *Bill hangs out with Donna and Leo and Terry.* Someone's probably saying those very words, right now.'

'So?' Terry said. 'We'll deny the lot. Give each other alibis, like we always planned.'

'But with the fire—' Donna's voice cracked suddenly and she sat down on the mattress. No need to spell out the rest. She'd burnt down two schools when she was thirteen and they'd caught her sprinkling paraffin in a third one. All the police had to do was check their records.

'The fire was a pretty dumb thing to do,' Terry said bitterly.

'But I didn't—I never—' Donna looked up at him, surprised and defiant, and for a second Nick felt that they were poised on the edge of a quarrel that would tear the whole situation apart.

Instead, Terry grabbed her by the shoulders. 'We've just got to stick together,' he said stubbornly. 'What've they got? Some old guy, with bad eyesight, who *thinks* he saw Bill's bike in the dark. That's nothing. They won't be able to touch us if we back each other up.'

'What about the kid?' Donna said in a thick voice, glaring at Nick.

'He's all right.' Terry clapped Nick on the back, so hard that he knocked the breath out of him. 'He'll stick by us, won't you, Nick? We're all in this together.' He grinned encouragingly, as if they were mates. Comrades, with the torchlight on their faces, standing back to back against the danger and the dark.

Only it was all wrong, and suddenly Nick knew why. Terry wasn't sure of the others at all. All this stuff about *We'll stick together, the way we planned* was all talk, all part of a game. It was no more real than the game Nick played with Ruth and Joseph. That was why Terry kept saying it so firmly, over and over again. He wanted somebody to say it back to him, so that he could believe in it.

Nick looked him straight in the eye and nodded. 'We're

all in this together. You can trust me.'

'Knew we could,' Terry said easily. But his breathing slowed down as he relaxed. 'Now all we've got to do is get hold of Leo and make sure we're all telling the same story. We have to be sure—'

'Terry!'

It was Mrs Miller's voice from downstairs, very loud and shrill. Terry looked at Nick. 'Thought she was out.'

'She was when I came in. Must have let herself in without us hearing.' Nick shrugged. 'So what?'

Then she called again—'*Terry!*'—and there was something in her voice that made them all go very still.

'Go on, kid.' Terry gave Nick a little push towards the door. 'See what she wants.'

Nick opened the door, walked across the landing, and looked down. Straight on to a policeman.

There were three of them standing in the hall, blocking the way to the front door, watching Mrs Miller as she came slowly up the stairs, still calling.

For a second, Nick's brain worked at top speed, uselessly hunting for a way to warn Terry, to get Donna out of the house, to get hold of Leo and tell him—

Then Mrs Miller said, 'You'd better put on some proper clothes, Terry. You've got visitors.'

Terry had come out of his bedroom to take a look at what was going on. The moment Mrs Miller spoke, one of the policemen was beside her on the stairs, keeping an eye on things, and when he saw who was behind Terry, in the room, he grinned as if things had taken a turn for the better.

'Hallo, Donna. Fancy seeing you here. We've just been round your house, talking to your mum.'

The policeman was taller than Terry or Donna and they suddenly looked young and awkward, scowling and shuffling their feet. Nick glared at the police, desperately trying to rearrange the scene in his head, to get back the feeling he'd had when he and Terry and the others had all set out on the bikes together.

*They're not policemen, they're orcs. Foul-smelling blue orcs, controlled by an evil overlord. They're ruthless and cruel, but they're stupid as well, and we can defeat them if only we keep faith and fight together. The heroes, the adventurers, can resist the power of evil and—*

But it was no use. They weren't orcs. They were policemen, and there was nothing heroic about the way Terry and Donna were facing them.

Nick was suddenly cold, so cold that he had to clench all his muscles to stop himself shivering. Fear shook him, choking off his breath. He was terrified that, at any moment, one of the policemen would notice his expression and grab him. *Now then, kid, what are you looking so scared about? Have you got anything to do with this little lot?*

But no one so much as glanced at him. He was only the little brother, standing watching. The policeman waited while Terry pulled on his jeans and a sweatshirt, and then he ushered Terry and Donna downstairs and into the front room, with Mrs Miller following.

Nick sat down on the top stair feeling foolish and helpless. He couldn't even phone Leo, to warn him, because the police might hear him talking in the hall. Leaning his head against the banisters, he stared at the closed door and listened to the voices murmuring behind it.

They didn't murmur for long. After ten minutes they all came trooping out again and Mrs Miller called up the stairs to Nick.

'We're just going out for a bit. Not sure how long we'll be. I'll phone Dad and tell him what's happened, but can you get yourself some tea?'

Nick could see that she was struggling not to cry and he nodded, to keep her happy. But he knew that he wouldn't be able to eat a thing. It was all he could do to breathe. He was still expecting one of the policemen to look up, suddenly, and say, 'Wait a moment. Wasn't there a kid riding pillion . . .?'

But nothing like that happened. His mother opened the door and walked down the path, and a policeman nodded at Terry and Donna to follow her to the car. Donna moved like a cat, very neat, very tense, but Terry shuffled like an old man with his shoulders drooping.

In spite of his terror, Nick was expecting some kind of

signal from Terry. Surely he would look up as he went, or make a gesture behind his back? But there was nothing. They all went out, the last policeman pulled the door shut, and Nick was left on his own, sitting looking down the stairs.

*We're all in this together.* The words rang in his head. Empty. Meaningless. If they were in it together, he should have been in the police car now, sitting shoulder to shoulder with Terry and Donna. Or else he should have been able to use his freedom to plan an escape for them. But there was nothing he could do. He was just a kid and the game had left him behind.

Slowly, just for the sake of doing something, he walked down to the front room, looked up Leo's number in the phone book and dialled it. Then he sat with the phone pressed to his ear, listening as it rang and rang and rang. He wasn't even going to be able to do that one little thing. He was *useless*.

Listlessly, he put the receiver down, walked out into the hall and climbed the stairs to his bedroom. He was cold, so very very cold. His whole body felt as if it was icing up.

Crawling into his bed, he pulled the covers over his head and lay still. It didn't matter what he did. It didn't matter to anyone. And all he wanted was to get *warm*.

He didn't know how long he lay there, but he must have fallen asleep eventually, because the phone woke him, ringing downstairs. On and on and on.

When he first realized what it was, he just pulled the covers higher over his head. He thought it was probably his father phoning to say he couldn't get back that night. And *he* didn't want to be the one to tell Dad what had happened.

But then it struck him that it might be Leo on the phone. Or even Bill, trying to find out what had happened to the others. He leapt up, scattering blankets, raced down the stairs and grabbed the receiver.

'Yeah?'

It was a phone box. He waited for the pips to stop and then spoke again, eagerly.

'Leo? Is that you?'

'I'm sorry?' The voice was female, vaguely familiar, and it sounded bewildered.

Nick was so stupid with shock, that he could not move his mind out of the groove it was in.

'Who's that? Are you Bill's mother?'

'Nick, is that you?' The voice sounded even more puzzled, and it was a girl's not a woman's. Definitely not anyone's mother.

'Oh. Sorry.'

'That *is* you, isn't it, Nick?' The voice was impatient now, and the sharpness suddenly brought the right face swimming up in his mind to match it.

'*Ruth!*'

# Chapter 20

'Ruth?' It was like a voice from a different world, a different life. She was the last person he wanted to talk to just then, and if he had not been slowed down by shock he would have hung up on her. But he replied automatically. 'What do you want?'

'I want you to meet me in McDonalds in half an hour. OK? There's something I've got to talk to you about.'

'What?' He couldn't take it in. Couldn't cope with anything else.

'McDonalds,' Ruth said, slowly, snapping the word out. 'In half an hour. Understand now?'

'Yes,' Nick said, meaning that he understood, not that he would come. But he never got a chance to explain that.

'Right,' Ruth said briskly, 'I'll see you there.' And she put the phone down.

*Oh no, you won't. You can sit in McDonalds until Christmas for all I care. I'm not having anything to do with any hypocritical Fishers. We've got enough trouble as it is.*

But then he thought of something else and his whole body went cold again. Suppose Ruth knew something? Suppose he'd left something in the shop, mixed up with the mess from the robbery. Something that Ruth recognized. What would she do about it?

His mind went wild, sketching out disasters. The Fishers were hopelessly hard up, after all. She was going to blackmail him. *Ten pounds a week, every week, or I'll tell the police.* Why not? If Joseph could set fire to the shop, Ruth could do anything, anything at all. And if he didn't meet her at McDonalds, all she had to do was walk down two blocks and go into the police station.

It was all there in his head, a lurid, dramatic picture. Ruth's face, screwed into a mean, bullying mask, her hand, stretched out palm uppermost with the fingers cupped. Fear made the images sharp and bright, and he was suddenly in a panic in case he failed to get to McDonalds in time. He had his bike out of the shed in a couple of minutes, and within a quarter of an hour he was sitting in front of a large milk shake and a packet of french fries, trying to ignore all the schoolkids who had taken the place over. He didn't feel as if he was waiting for Ruth. He felt as if he was waiting for a monster.

She came punctually, exactly half an hour after she had put the phone down. Her baggy old coat hung round her and her hair was twisted firmly into a tight plait. While she was buying a single small cup of coffee at the counter, everyone at the tables stared curiously at her.

Nick looked across and caught her eye as she came towards him. 'So what's up?' he said roughly, the moment she was close enough.

Ruth glared at him and looked around, but Mandy Brogan had just walked in wearing fluorescent green shorts and no one was taking much notice of anything else. Ruth relaxed and slid into the seat opposite Nick.

'Come on,' he said, determined not to let her get the upper hand. 'You've dragged me here without giving me a reason. The least you can do is explain.'

Ruth took a very small, frugal sip of her coffee. Then she said, 'Did you see Joseph at school today?'

Nick blinked. All that business of yelling and waving the pictures seemed a million years ago. If Ruth just wanted to smack his wrists for being a naughty boy, she was going to get an earful. 'So what if I did?'

The tone of his voice made her frown, but she didn't snap back. Instead, she leaned closer, lowering her voice. 'Did you think he was—peculiar?'

Nick scowled. 'Of course he was peculiar. You're all peculiar, aren't you? Your whole rotten family.'

Even then she didn't join in the fight. She gave a quick, backward flick of her left hand, as if she were brushing away something too unimportant to discuss. 'Look, I'm sorry about what happened on Monday, in the game. But you *must* see that doesn't mean anything now. Not after what's happened to us.'

*Come on*, said her expression. *Quit the quarrel. Talk grown-up talk.* Nick sulked a second longer and then gave in. At least she wasn't trying to blackmail him. He shrugged and gave an answer off the top of his head, careful not to say anything incriminating.

'OK, so Joseph was odd. Just like you'd expect a person to be when his home's burnt down.'

'But don't you see?' Ruth banged her fist on the table so hard that three or four people looked round. 'That's just it. He's miserable, absolutely miserable. But the rest of us can't even pretend to be, because—'

For a second Nick was puzzled, and then he got it. She didn't know, of course. She thought it was the gang who had set fire to the shop, and so she couldn't understand why her darling brother wasn't grinning up his sleeve, like the rest of them.

Ruth went on without waiting for him to answer. 'Mr Pollitt gave him a lift over to Gran's. He came through the front door and just stood looking at us all. Then he said, "We've been burgled and the shop's on fire." Quite quietly, as if it was nothing special.'

'And the rest of you jumped up and sang the Hallelujah Chorus, I suppose?'

Ruth's mouth trembled suddenly. 'If you'd seen Dad's *face!* About half the wrinkles vanished, just like that, as if he'd relaxed for the first time in ten years. He said, "We mustn't be glad because someone else has done wrong," but it wasn't any use. Everyone was smiling, and Gran squeezed Mum's hand and whispered, "Well, I shouldn't say it, I know, but God looks after his own." And all the time, there was Joseph—'

Nick closed his eyes and swallowed. 'Shock.'

'Well, that's what we all thought, of course, and Dad took him in to the hospital so they could look him over. But—' Ruth frowned and took another, microscopic sip of coffee. 'It's almost a week now, and he hasn't changed. Won't talk to me, doesn't listen to anything you say— there's something wrong, Nick.'

*There sure is, and if you knew what it was, it would send you out of your mind.* Nick pushed his packet of french fries across the table towards her. 'So why come and talk to me? What do you want me to do about it?'

135

Ruth took a chip and stared down at it, as though she didn't recognize it as food. 'Well, partly I thought you might understand. Because you're the only real friend Joseph's got.'

It wasn't an accusation, but Nick suddenly felt guilty. He *was* the only person who could possibly understand how Joseph felt. The only person in the whole world. But why should he—?

'What do you want me to do about it?' he said again, but differently. Not angrily.

Ruth looked up and gave him a small, grateful smile. 'I thought perhaps—if we played the game. I think, if we did that, I could work out a way of getting him to talk. That's what he needs, Nick. Something's bottled up inside him, I know it is, and he's got to let it out.'

*You'll get a lot more than you bargain for.* Nick hesitated, not sure of what he felt. Then he suddenly remembered Donna's face. Terry being taken away by the police. The guilt of watching them go, and knowing they would get done for the fire as well as the robbery.

But Joseph had *meant* to start the fire.

The temptation jumped out at Nick. There was no way he could explain to anyone what had happened. Not without incriminating himself. But if Joseph confessed to the fire . . . Ruth wouldn't let him keep it secret. The moment she knew, she'd have him down at the police station, singing his little song, Nick was certain. No cover-ups for the Fishers. She would make Joseph claim responsibility, and that would let Terry and the others off the hook, at least as far as the fire was concerned. Very neat.

'We-ell,' he said, not wanting to sound too keen.

'Please, Nick.' Ruth looked desperate. 'I know it will work.'

'You want me to come round to—' Nick remembered that they couldn't be at home, '—to wherever you are?'

Ruth almost smiled. 'To where we're staying? I don't think the Pollitts would fancy that. Anyway, there's no room. But if we could come to your house—'

Nick's mind juggled pictures of his mum, the police, the two Fishers. 'I'm not sure.'

'Oh, come on. We don't need a wardrobe or anything. Just a room with thick curtains, where we won't be disturbed.'

'You can try if you like,' Nick said. 'But I don't think you'll get Joseph round to our house. He—we had a sort of row at school today.'

Ruth looked hard at him, but why should he tell her what had happened? He returned her stare, with interest.

'You leave that side of it to me,' she said at last. 'All you need to do is play when I get him round there. Tomorrow evening?'

'OK, but—'

Before Nick could finish his sentence, there was a yodel from the doorway.

'Oy-oy-oy, what's this then? Got a new girl-friend, Miller? Didn't know you fancied older women.' Parker looked a bit lost on his own, and he was struggling to keep up his usual brand of chatter as he crossed the room towards them.

'Push off,' Nick said.

'Oh, come on,' said Parker pettishly. 'I don't know what's got into you lot. Livingstone bit my head off when I went round to his house, and now you're at it.'

He glanced pathetically at Ruth, looking for a bit of support, but she hardly noticed him. Standing up, as if there was no point in waiting now she'd done what she came for, she drained her coffee to the bottom of the cup. Then she nodded briskly at Nick and walked out.

Parker leered at him. 'Looks like you haf been stood up, darleenk. How you say we spend the evenink togezzer? Ve could wandalize a few—how you say?—phone boxes?'

'I've got better things to do,' Nick said gruffly, and walked out.


But when he got home, he was sorry he hadn't accepted Parker's offer. His mother and father were up in Terry's room, packing a bag for him, and he heard his dad complaining, at top volume, the moment he walked in.

'Bloody ridiculous not giving him bail. What do they

137

think he's going to do? Hop on Concorde?'

Nick looked at his mother. 'They've charged him?'

She nodded. 'All of them.'

'Have they got Bill as well?'

His mother suddenly went very still, with a pair of socks dangling in one hand, and Nick realized that the question was a dead giveaway. It showed he knew exactly how many of Terry's gang had been on the raid. The innocent little brother wasn't such an innocent after all.

He watched her take it in—and then deliberately wipe it out of her mind. Her face went blank and she turned away and went on putting socks in the bag. Just for a second, Nick wished she had grabbed him by the collar and shaken the truth out of him. But there was none of that. She was desperate not to talk about it, and so was his father.

And that was how it went on. For the next twenty-four hours, they nearly broke their necks avoiding the subject of the raid and the gang. The three of them smiled brightly at each other and talked about the weather or the news or the football results. Nick felt as if he was wrapped in cottonwool.

It was just as bad at school. Livingstone was avoiding the subject too, and he refused to be left alone with Nick. Every time Nick walked into a room, Livingstone made an excuse to leave it, as if there was no other way to avoid talking about the arrests.

Nick was in the middle of the silences, with the key to everything. The only person who knew exactly what had happened. And all day the truth danced round and round in his head, spiky with questions he couldn't answer.

*Decide, decide,* a voice in his head kept whispering. *You have the power to decide who gets convicted. You're the only one who knows the truth.* But how did people ever make these Great Decisions? It was like trying to grab hold of a piece of wet soap. The harder he clutched at it, the faster it slipped away from him.

# Chapter 21

By the evening, Nick was totally confused. He had run over everything in his head so often that he couldn't think about it at all. If he tried to work out what to do, his brain simply shut off and turned away to something else.

And that was how Ruth managed to pull a fast one on him.

He hadn't really expected that she would get Joseph to come. But at eight o'clock sharp the doorbell rang, and there they both were when he opened the door.

'Ah.' Nick stared, too surprised even to ask them in for a moment.

Joseph looked carefully at him, as if he were waiting for something. When Nick didn't speak, he said gruffly, 'Ruth told me you wanted to talk.'

'I—' Nick glanced at her, but she didn't bat an eyelid.

'I told Joseph that it wasn't fair not to give you a chance to apologize. That you'd said you were ready to play again.'

Very cunning. Every word was good solid truth, but Ruth had arranged it to sound as if Nick was begging for forgiveness. He hesitated, wondering whether to tell them to push off and slam the door in their faces but in that instant, before he could get the words out, Ruth walked past him into the hall, swinging her plastic carrier bag.

'How about if I go and get ready to play while you two sort things out?'

The sitting-room door opened a crack and a shadow flickered behind it. Mum on the watch. Nick pulled himself together. He had to get Ruth and Joseph out of the way, before she found out who they were.

'Top of the stairs,' he said. 'Last room at the end of the landing.'

'Fine. Give me ten minutes.'

She was halfway up the stairs before she had finished speaking. Joseph and Nick followed her, more slowly, and stood on the landing, staring at each other.

Nick's first thought was that Ruth was dead right about Joseph being peculiar. He didn't smile or look round the place or ask what on earth Nick had been up to, waving Livingstone's pictures under his nose. He simply stood, passively, and waited for the next thing to happen.

For a second, Nick was shocked. Almost upset to see him like that. Then a harder, colder feeling took over. Joseph was the one who'd gone on at him about maps and rules and trying to be good. The one who'd said Thomas had to suffer for *stealing* the keys. He *deserved* to suffer himself.

'Is it OK where you're staying?' he said at last, just to break the silence.

'It was nice of the Pollitts to take us in,' Joseph said listlessly, as if it could have been a dungeon for all he cared.

'Oh well.' Nick looked sympathetic. 'It's not for long, is it? Only until the insurance people pay up.' Pow! Straight to the jaw! Joseph turned pale and Nick had to remind himself that he couldn't afford to be sympathetic. He had to concentrate on protecting himself.

Then the ten minutes had passed. Nick switched off the landing light and tapped on his bedroom door.

'Ready,' said Ruth, in her Jezebel voice.

As Nick pushed the door open, he smelt the familiar, smoky-rose scent of the incense sticks. They stood in the far corner of the room, dull orange pinpricks of light, clustered on top of the chest of drawers.

Ruth hadn't bothered with trying to hide or shut herself away. She was sitting in the darkness, in front of the window, with the curtains carefully arranged so that a narrow band of sky showed between them. The angle of her head and the shape of her piled-up hair were just the same as always and Nick felt a shudder tingle up his spine, as if he had opened his bedroom door and walked into another place.

'We'll sit on the bed.' He pushed Joseph across and dragged the bedside table round in front of them. 'Have you got the torch and the map?'

'Of course.' Joseph's voice was dull, but he took the things out and arranged them in front of him in a row, the lighted torch turned towards the two of them. Pencil, pens, rubber, map, dice. And the little dwarf figure, which he stood in the centre of the table.

Nick pulled his Star Warrior out of his pocket, hesitated, and then put it down a few inches away from the dwarf, with a clear space between them.

'What do we do now?'

Joseph shrugged. 'Ask her. She'll make sure you do what she wants.'

Every word came out as though it was a giant effort, and Nick shoved his hands into his pockets, to stop them shaking Joseph. Then he started, experimentally.

'What is your will, O Queen?'

'The spider is dead,' said the voice from across the room. 'The blood price must be paid.'

It was all Nick could do not to laugh out loud. *The spider*. When he thought of all that had happened since, it seemed ridiculous to be making a fuss about a little thing like that. But a game was a game, so he played along.

'What is the blood price? What must I pay?'

'Not you alone. The whole company must pay for the sins of the company.'

Oh ho. Nick thought he had a sniff of her plan. He nudged Joseph. 'Is that right? Do you have to pay too?'

'Suppose so,' Joseph said, as though it didn't interest him much. 'I've never played with anyone else before, have I?'

'All right,' Nick said, speaking to Ruth. 'What do we do? What are our options?'

'You have no options yet. As the blood of the spider sinks into the earth you, Zephaniah, hear the feet of orcs approaching from both ends of the tunnel. They have scented the death. There is no escape from them.'

'And Jethro?' Nick asked it, because Joseph showed no signs of speaking.

'Jethro is caught instantly. A net falls from the roof of the tunnel, where he stands waiting for you, and he is tangled in meshes that he cannot see.'

'And the orcs get me too?'

Across the room, the head with its piled hair nodded slowly. 'You are both bound tightly, gagged and blindfolded. The orcs carry you fast along twisting tunnels, until you have lost all sense of where you are and which way you are going.'

Joseph moved suddenly. Nick saw him lay down his pencil and push the map book away from him. For some reason, that was very satisfying, but Nick did not comment.

'You are laid down at last,' Ruth went on, 'and your legs are untied so that you can stand. But the blindfolds remain. Turn off the torch and cover your eyes with your hands.'

Joseph's fingers reached out and clicked the switch of the torch. *Stupid to make us cover our eyes as well*, thought Nick. *What's the point, when it's dark already?* But as he pressed his palms to his eyes, the double dark seemed to wrap itself round him, to seep inside his head.

Then there was silence. It was thirty seconds before Ruth spoke again, and when she did, her voice was slow and heavy. 'Now you stand before me in my judgement hall. One of my servants has been unjustly killed, and you are guilty. Do you dispute your guilt?'

Nick considered for a moment. No. There was nothing to be gained by that. 'I admit it freely.'

'Then you must pay the blood price.'

'What price must we pay?' Nick said, suddenly very tense. This must be it. This *had* to be it. But how was she going to con a confession out of Joseph?

He heard her take a deep breath. 'You must pay with truth,' she said slowly. 'Truth is the only thing that can be accepted in exchange for life. Each of you must tell me his closest, most fiercely guarded secret.'

*No!* Nick was so disappointed that he nearly shouted it aloud. That wasn't enough, not nearly enough to get Joseph to give up *his* crucial secret. Peering sideways, between his fingers, he saw that Joseph had taken his hands away from his eyes and was fiddling with his pencil, deliberately trying to escape from the tension that Ruth had built up. It wasn't going to work.

But it had to! Desperately, Nick searched his mind for something he could do, something that would take the tension up a notch and force the truth out of Joseph. Something as important as his precious secret, so that he couldn't ignore it. But not—

'Speak,' said the voice from across the room.

And suddenly Nick realized that he had the lever he needed, ready in his hands. It was perfectly simple. He could get the truth out of Joseph without giving himself away at all. Picking up his Star Warrior, he spoke the words harshly, without working out what he was going to say.

'All right, I'll tell you something true. A secret that my family is keeping. My brother has been arrested and they've charged him with being in the gang that burnt down your shop. He's going to get done for robbery. *And arson.*'

Snap.

The pencil broke between Joseph's fingers. For a second the air was so thick with silence that Nick nearly choked on it. Then, from beside him, came a fast, stumbling voice.

'When I walked into the shop, I saw it was all turned upside down, and I could smell the paraffin. It was like hearing a voice in my head. Matches, matches, matches . . . On and on and on. And I thought—'

Joseph stopped. Gulped a huge, noisy breath of air. Then he shouted the last words into the darkness.

'It was a mistake, it was all a mistake. *I thought what I was doing was right!*'

Right, wrong, right, wrong . . .

The room spun at Nick, as if Joseph's voice had set it whirling. He was there in the wrecked shop again, with the smashed window and the paraffin smell, and the bikes starting up outside. Feeling the matchsticks between his fingers. Scraping them against the box.

Suppose there really were no rules at all? The world rocked around him, threatening to disintegrate. He didn't want the explanation, didn't want to hear what Joseph was going to say.

'Stop!' He yelled, very loud. The only way to keep things under control was to wreck the game. Turn Jezebel back into Ruth and pull them out of the darkness.

Still clutching his Star Warrior, he pushed past Joseph, sent the stool flying, and grabbed at the light switch. That was it. The moment the light was on, Jezebel would only be Ruth draped in dressing-up clothes, and the blood price for

143

the spider would just be part of a game that they had stopped playing.

He flicked the light on and, while he was still blinking from the sudden brightness, turned and saw—Jezebel.

Oh, the clothes were jumble sale tat all right. An emerald-green evening dress, stained down the front, and a black cloak made out of a curtain. But the face was real and the accusing eyes were terrifying under the green-painted eyelids. Steady and stern and relentless. Turning the light on hadn't ruined the game at all. It had simply moved it into reality.

It was only for a second that they stayed like that, one of those seconds that went on for ever, as if everyone's blood had stopped flowing. Then Joseph jumped up and bolted through the door, and Ruth stretched out her hands, with the glass-studded rings glinting on every finger, and screeched at Nick.

'Stop him!'

# Chapter 22

Nick reacted faster than he knew he could. He was up and out of the room so quickly that he managed to catch up halfway down the stairs. Shoving his arm round Joseph's throat, to keep him quiet, he hissed in his ear.

'Knock it off, you fool! Calm down, or the police will have it all sewn up before you've had time to think.'

Mr and Mrs Miller were still in the sitting room, and they must have heard the scuffle outside. Mr Miller was there before Joseph could answer, peering round the door at them.

'Nick?'

Nick still had the Star Warrior in his hand, and he tapped Joseph on the head with it, to show that they were only kidding about. 'Just come down to make a cup of coffee. Want one?'

Mr Miller looked hard at them for a second and then he shook his head. 'No thanks. Just had one.' And he disappeared back behind the door.

'That's not a bad idea, either.' Nick let go of Joseph's throat and grabbed his wrist instead. 'Let's go and make ourselves some.'

Joseph came like a zombie and sat down at the kitchen table with his head in his hands, while Nick set up the coffee maker and fetched the mugs. When Nick pushed a mug of coffee at him, he reached for it and spoke without raising his head.

'I really did it, you know. I set the shop on fire. I found the floor covered with paraffin, but I was the one who lit the matches.'

'Yes,' Nick said, not looking at him. 'I know.'

Joseph nodded three times, very slowly. 'It was only a couple of seconds, when I first came into the shop. Suddenly everything seemed very clear. All I had to do was light a few matches and we'd be out of the whole wretched tangle. It was like hearing a good, strong voice telling me to do it. Just for those few seconds, I really thought it was *right*.'

Nick remembered how Joseph had closed his eyes and bent his head. 'I know,' he said.

'So what do I do now?'

It was the question that had been haunting Nick all day. His eyes slid away. 'You could just shut up and take the money. Most people would.'

Joseph's mouth twisted into a smile that looked as though it hurt. 'I thought that was going to be my punishment. Knowing what I'd done and having to keep quiet about it. But I can't. It won't work.'

'Because of Terry's gang being caught?'

'Not just that.' Joseph shook his head. 'That's important too, of course, but I'd made up my mind before you told me that, I think.'

'So why?' Nick said. 'Why mess everything up if it was working out right?'

'But it's *not* right, is it?' Joseph said miserably. 'Nothing can change that. If I let it go on happening, the whole world will be—wrong. And that would be even worse than losing the shop and paying back the insurance money.'

'Paying back the—' Nick goggled at him. 'Why should you pay it back? You've lost the shop.'

'You think Dad would take the money now, even if they offer it?' Joseph said, every word sharp and hard. 'When I got it by doing wrong?'

'But it wasn't wrong!' Nick banged the table so hard that the Star Warrior fell over. 'You can't have been doing something wrong if you thought it was right. Like you said, it was a mistake.'

'Of course it was wrong,' Joseph said fiercely. He was twisting his fingers as he talked, digging his nails into the flesh. 'Right and wrong don't *change*, you know. They're like a map, to stop people making—mistakes. If I'd looked at the map, I would have known that the voice in my head was just me, wanting the easy way out.'

Nick thought of Thomas, playing happily. Of little Susie, and their tired, grey parents. If they lost the insurance money as well as the shop, they would all be homeless.

146

'Is it really worth it?' he said furiously. 'Giving up everything—making your family give up everything—just to "do what's right"?'

Joseph looked down at his fingers. 'I think so.'

'You're crazy!' Nick banged the table with his fist.

Joseph didn't answer. Didn't try to argue. For a minute he sat there with his head bent, staring down at the table, and then he stood up.

'Is it OK if I use the phone?'

Nick's chest was so tight that he could hardly breathe, but he forced the words out somehow. 'Help yourself.'

Joseph walked out into the hall and picked up the receiver. His hands must have been shaking, because he misdialled the Pollitts' number twice. The third time, when he got through and asked for his father, his face was as pale as paper and Nick could see his breathing quicken. It seemed indecent to sit there and watch him, but clumsy to move or shut the door.

Just as Joseph started to say, 'Dad? I'm afraid I've got something to tell you—' Ruth came padding down the stairs. She had scrubbed the make-up off her face and changed into her ordinary clothes, but her hair was loose and wild round her shoulders.

'The moment I've told you,' Joseph said into the receiver, 'I'm off to the police station.'

Ruth slid quickly into the kitchen and shut the door behind her.

'Got more than you bargained for, didn't you?' Nick said bitterly. 'What took you so long? Couldn't you face coming down to pick up the pieces?'

Ruth glanced over her shoulder, towards the closed door. 'He's going through with it, then? He's going to confess?'

Nick nodded, watching her to see whether she understood all that Joseph's confession would mean. She understood perfectly. For a second she stood very still, not moving a muscle. Then she said, 'Well,' very softly. Nothing else.

'Nobody made him do it,' Nick said, too fast and too loud. 'He knows he's making you all homeless.'

Slowly Ruth sat down on the chair that Joseph had just

147

left, spreading her hands on the table and looking down at her nails. 'I've been thinking,' she said. It was a quiet voice, not like her usual sharp one. 'I've been thinking everything over very carefully while I was getting changed.'

Suddenly, for no real reason, Nick felt cold. He turned away and began to make her a cup of coffee, so that he would have a reason not to look at her. 'Congratulations.'

She ignored the sarcasm and went on, still quietly. 'That gang who did the shop over—they weren't just a crowd of hooligans out on the rampage. They knew things. Private things. Like when we'd all be out, and where the keys were, and how to find the safe. The kind of thing you only find out by knowing somewhere. Visiting and talking and helping out.' She swallowed, as if her throat had gone dry. 'And playing with the kids.'

Her expression was like the one on her face when she came in and found him playing burglars with Thomas. Nick's hands were clammy as he poured the coffee. 'That's what you think?'

'You were too good just now, while we were playing the game,' Ruth said. He could only just hear her. 'You knew exactly how to get Joseph to talk, because you knew what he was hiding. And the only way you could have known that—'

'He might have told me,' Nick said quickly. 'Or Terry might have seen him light the fire and told me afterwards.'

Ruth didn't bother to argue. They both knew that neither of those explanations would work.

Nick slopped milk into her mug and banged it down on the table in front of her. 'OK, if you're so sure I was involved, you go and tell your fancy stories to the police.'

'You've got me wrong.' Ruth stood up, ignoring the coffee. 'It's not revenge I'm after. I've got a different weakness.'

'So what *do* you want?'

For a split second, so quickly that he hardly saw it, the corner of her mouth twitched. 'I like to know about people. And I particularly like to know what they'll do when they're up against it. When they have to make decisions, work out the right thing to do. That's what it's all about, after all, isn't it?'

She picked up the Star Warrior and stood him neatly on his feet, in the centre of the table. All on his own.

'There you are. If you want to go on playing Sir Nick, the Stainless Superhero, that's your business. I'm going down to the police station with Joseph.'

She walked out of the door, just as Joseph put the phone down. Nick saw them glance at each other and grin quickly, each encouraging the other. Then they had gone, and he was left remembering the look on their faces and the sound of Terry's voice.

*He'll stick by us, won't you, Nick? We're all in this together.*

It was like being stabbed with a small, sharp dagger. Picking up the teaspoons from his cup and Joseph's, he threaded them between his fingers. Everyone was down at the police station. Terry and Donna and Leo and Bill. And now Joseph and Ruth as well. He was the only one left, and Ruth thought he ought to join the rest of them.

But she didn't know what she was asking.

He knew he would never stand up to being questioned. If the police started on him he would tell them everything. And he'd land up with a conviction for arson, just like Donna.

It wasn't as though he'd done anything really wrong . . .

Then he thought of the Fishers, with nowhere to live, because Mr Fisher wouldn't take the insurance money if Joseph had started the fire.

But then he thought about his own mum and dad, and how they'd feel, seeing him in court pleading guilty.

Every time he latched on to one argument, he thought of another to knock it on the head. It was like being out on the Marsh in a thick fog, with shapes looming and disappearing. Signposts and houses and hedges dissolving as he tried to reach them. And the ground underfoot shifting treacherously so that everything moved and cracked and slid . . . Nowhereland.

Slowly he put down the teaspoons he was holding in front of the Star Warrior. Laid them carefully so that they stretched out like two shining silver paths, one going right and one going left. Then he squatted down, to get his face at the same level as the model's, so that the paths stretched in front of him too.

*OK. Which way are you going? How do you make the choice, Zephaniah?*

Suddenly, sharp in his mind, he saw the faces. Faces in the torchlight, shadowed and stern, trusting each other because that was the only way to survive. Joseph and Ruth. Terry, Leo, Donna and Bill. The company of adventurers.

At last he understood, dimly, how that trust came about. It wasn't something you could think of when it suited you and ignore for the rest of the time, like the rules of a game. It had to be built, slowly and painfully, brick by brick, out of actions that really mattered. Something that could take your whole life. But—what was it Ruth had said? *That's what it's all about, after all, isn't it?*

Picking up the Star Warrior, he slipped it into his pocket and walked through the kitchen door into the hall. For a moment he hesitated there, looking at the closed door of the sitting room where his parents were. Joseph had phoned his father first, to let him know what was happening. Staring at the door, Nick knew that he was not that strong. He would give in if his mother pleaded. And that wouldn't get rid of the suffering. It would simply move back to Joseph's family.

Very quietly, he walked out and closed the front door after him. Joseph and Ruth were halfway down the hill and for a moment he stood at the gate, watching them walking side by side with the pale winter sun on their hair.

He felt as if he was walking into the entrance of a tunnel, with only a vague idea of where it might lead him. Away from Livingstone and Parker, that was for sure. Closer to Joseph and Ruth. And at the end of the tunnel?

It was impossible to guess that. The only thing he knew was that, at last, he really was stepping out into real life. He'd come to the end of playing games.

Slowly he pushed the gate open, feeling the roughness of the wood against his fingers and hearing the old, familiar squeak that would never be quite the same again. It was his last chance. The last opportunity to change his mind.

He decided. Stepping through the gate, he let it bang shut behind him and ran down the hill towards Ruth and Joseph. Hearing the sound of his feet, they looked back and stopped to wait for him, with the sunlight full on their faces.